Ben Bova is editor of *Analog* and author of a number of works, including *Millennium*. (also available in Orbit).

Aliens

3 Novellas
edited by
Ben Bova

Futura Publications Ltd
An Orbit Book

An Orbit Book

Edited by Ben Bova
Associate Editors:
Peter Weston and Victoria Schochet

First published in Great Britain by
Futura Publications Limited in 1977

ISBN 0 8600 7958 9

Printed by
William Collins Sons & Co. Ltd
Glasgow

Futura Publications Limited
110 Warner Road, Camberwell
London SE5

CONTENTS

ACKNOWLEDGEMENTS

FIRST CONTACT by Murray Leinster copyright © 1945 by Street & Smith Publications Inc. Reprinted by permission of A. M. Heath & Company Limited.

THE BIG FRONT YARD by Clifford Simak copyright © 1958 Street & Smith Publications Inc. Reprinted by permission of the author.

A MEETING WITH MEDUSA by Arthur C. Clarke copyright © 1961 by Playboy Enterprises Inc. Reprinted by permission of the author and the author's agents, Scott Meredith Literary Agency Inc., 845 Third Avenue, New York, NY10022.

INTRODUCTION

By Ben Bova

In the Army they teach you that you don't salute the man, you salute the uniform. For me to be introducing Clifford D. Simak, Murray Leinster, and Arthur C. Clarke . . . well, it makes me feel like a shavetail lieutenant sauntering past a trio of grizzled, battle-wise veterans.

It has been my pleasure to meet each of these gentlemen, and to work with each of them. But before I bog down in personal reminiscences, there is some official business to get out of the way.

This book is the first in a series that will feature the most distinguished writers in the science fiction field, and their most distinguished stories. More than that: Futura Publications' THREE BY series represents a solution to a problem that has, for decades, nagged science fiction editors and impoverished science fiction readers.

The problem is simply this: how can we anthologize novellas?

Unless you are intimately familiar with the publishing business and its peculiar institutions, the question may mean nothing to you. So let me explain.

Science fiction is probably the most difficult form of literature to write. Isaac Asimov, who has written just about everything, assures me that this is true, so it must be so. In a science fiction story, the author must not only accomplish all the characterizations, mood, style, and plot of any type of story; he (or she) must in addition describe to the reader a whole new world, one that has never existed before, a world that is the invention of the author and has never been seen by anyone else.

Thus, when an author writes a contemporary story and says

that the hero took a bus from home to office, the reader can immediately visualize the situation. Even in an historical novel, when the hero rides his foaming stallion from manor house to castle wall, the reader can still picture the scene quite clearly.

But how does the author make the reader *see* what's going on when the hero teleports from a lunar colony to an interstellar ship cruising beyond 61 Cygni at nearly the speed of light? The author must show the reader, in some little detail, every aspect of the scene – because none of it is familiar, none of it based on the common pool of experience that the author and the reader share.

This need to build every detail of a story carefully, painstakingly, and yet entertainingly – so that the reader is not put off by dull lectures on engineering or astrophysics – places an additional burden on the writer of science fiction. A burden that does not exist for any other kind of writer.

It also tends to make science fiction stories longer and more elaborately detailed than most other types of fiction.

As a writer, I have often found it most difficult to produce a science fiction short story that is more meaningful than a sketch. As an editor, I see every day how tough it is for other writers to turn out strong short stories in the science fiction genre.

The best science fiction stories are often of lengths far greater than that of a short story. Many of the very best science fiction stories ever written are of a length that book publishers find almost impossible to deal with – from 20,000 to 40,000 words long.

They are usually called novellas, meaning short novels. Sometimes they are called novelettes, which is a term that generally connotes an extended short story. The two forms overlap in word-length, but not in style or treatment. The novella *is* a minor novel; its only difference from a full-blown novel is that it is less than the 60,000-word length that publishers usually require as a minimum for an individual book. The novelette is a long short story, in form, or sometimes a pair of interlocked short stories.

A story of twenty or thirty thousand words presents a problem for a book publisher. The story is too short to be published by itself; it is not 'book length'. Yet it is often too long for an anthology; it would take up nearly half the anthology's pages, and force the anthologist to drop several short stories to make room for one novella. Since anthologies are frequently sold on the strength of the contributors' names, it has become common wisdom to give the readers as many stories – hence as many authors – as possible.

Thus the novella is frequently homeless, relegated to publication in a magazine or in the occasional collection of stories by a single author.

The THREE BY series is intended to correct this unhappy situation. Each book of this series will include three novellas (or, in some cases, novelettes) that are acknowledged classics in the science fiction field, by authors who are acknowledged masters. Yet because of the mechanical problems discussed above, the novellas and novelettes in the THREE BY series have rarely been published in anthologies before.

Thanks to Futura Publications' dedication to presenting excellent science fiction, and to solving 'the novella problem', you can look forward to reading classic science fiction stories that have been virtually unobtainable for years.

And now, about the authors.

There is no point in introducing their stories, because the stories will speak for themselves far better than any introductory remarks can.

Instead of speaking about the stories, then, let me give you a look at a few key incidents that, I think, illuminate the mind and personality of each of these fine writers.

Gentleman is the word that comes easiest to mind when I think of Clifford Simak. A gentle man. At the Nebula Awards banquet of the Science Fiction Writers of America in New York, 30 April 1977, Cliff Simak was the featured speaker. Most of those present knew that he was to receive a special

Grand Master Nebula Award, an honour that had previously been bestowed only upon Robert A. Heinlein and Jack Williamson. Cliff, a veteran news reporter, must have had an inkling that he was going to receive the Grand Master tribute, but he never embarrassed anyone by letting on that he suspected. He wouldn't spoil our fun.

During his speech he was as nervous as a high school valedictorian. He is not a public man. After half a century as a newspaperman, he is still basically shy. He confessed that he had nothing very exciting to say, and then he spoke about his work in the science fiction field – the problems he faced, the times of disappointment and trial, the frustrations. He mentioned also the rewards of his work: not awards and honours, but friendships that have lasted through the decades, and the quiet pride of accomplishment.

By the time he finished his ten-minute speech, there was hardly a dry eye among that rather tough-minded audience of science fiction professionals.

I would like to think that if a space warp does open up, somewhere on Earth, and intelligent alien creatures step through it to inspect our planet and weigh the worth of its citizenry, the warp will be Cliff Simak's front yard – however large or small that may be. If it is, then I know that our race will be well represented.

I met Murray Leinster only once.

For years I had read his stories, and had known that Will F. Jenkins (his real name) was one of the last and best independent inventors in the United States. His inquisitive mind ranged over many different areas, but in his last years most of his work centred on aspects of photography. He invented, for example, a front-projection system for use in motion picture work that was the forerunner of the uncannily 'real' projections used in the Clarke/Kubrick masterwork, '2001: A Space Odessey'.

Mr Jenkins telephoned the *Analog* office shortly after I had become editor of the magazine, and told me that he would be in New York the following week. I immediately invited him to lunch.

Once we met, it was apparent that he was not in robust health. He had just recovered from a long siege of illness. The death of his wife had hurt him deeply. Yet he was alert, inquisitive, and full of ideas. He showed me a piece of film he was working on: it was both a positive and a negative, depending on the angle of the light falling upon it. At lunch we talked mainly about John Campbell, whom we both revered, and about Murray Leinster's stories, which went back as far as 1912, predating the earliest science fiction magazines.

After lunch was finished and we were bidding farewell to each other, he remarked with a grin, 'You know, we've been talking to each other for several hours now, and neither one of us has come up with a single brilliant idea!'

I don't think he was entirely joking. He expected brilliant ideas to arise every few hours, either from his own mind or from those around him. Certainly, with John Campbell, he must have met his match in creativity.

To this day, whenever I lean back in my desk chair and admire the awards that *Analog* has gathered, I can still hear Murray Leinster whispering to me, 'Remember Caesar, thou art mortal!'

What can I say about Arthur Clarke that hasn't already been said? Plenty.

In 1956, when Arthur Clarke visited the Martin Aircraft Co., where I was a junior technical editor on the *Vanguard* satellite launching project, I was given the happy task of ushering Arthur through the project, making certain that he got all the information he needed for the book he was doing on 'man's first artificial satellite'. Before he left the premises, I had the gall to push a three-hundred-page manuscript of mine on to him. The inevitable first novel. And he had the kindness to take it all the way back to his home in Ceylon, read it, and mail it back to me with a long letter of stern advice and gentle encouragement.

I remember driving Arthur through a New Jersey fog one dismal night, years later, crawling along at five miles per hour, desperately trying to see past the car's hood ornament, while he blithely chatted about *real* fogs in London!

We have met many times over the past twenty-some years, but my favourite meeting came in 1976, in Washington, D.C. That awful first manuscript I had palmed off on him twenty years earlier had finally grown into a published book, titled *Millennium.* I gave Arthur one of the first copies off the press, and thanked him for reading the earliest version of the novel.

'I read what?' he asked, incredulous. 'I never read other people's manuscripts. Never!'

And with that, he pulled a printed sheet of paper out of his briefcase, scribbled my name at its top, and presented it to me. It was a form letter, explaining that he simply doesn't have the time to read and comment on other people's manuscripts.

I treasure that form letter. And the longer, more personal letter he sent to me in 1956.

Now you know something about how and why this book came into being, and about the writers who have contributed to it. It is time to mention two very important persons whose names do not appear elsewhere.

I want to express my gratitude to Anthony J. V. Cheetham, of Futura Publications Ltd, who originated the idea for the THREE BY series, and to Victoria Schochet, my Associate Editor at *Analog* magazine, who did most of the real work connected with this book. Without them, this book could never have come into being.

Ben Bova
Manhattan
May 1977

FIRST CONTACT

by Murray Leinster

An expedition from Earth had gone to investigate the Crab Nebula. And – an expedition from Somewhere was already there! Now what is a spaceship skipper to do under such circumstances? Lead the possibly-deadly aliens home? Try to destroy them? What can he do?

I

Tommy Dort went into the captain's room with his last pair of stereophotos and said:

'I'm through, sir. These are the last two pictures I can take.'

He handed over the photographs and looked with professional interest at the visiplates which showed all space outside the ship. Subdued, deep-red lighting indicated the controls and such instruments as the quartermaster on duty needed for navigation of the spaceship *Llanvabon*. There was a deeply cushioned control chair. There was the little gadget of oddly angled mirrors – remote descendant of the back-view mirrors of twentieth-century motorists – which allowed a view of all the visiplates without turning the head. And there were the huge plates which were so much more satisfactory for a direct view of space.

The *Llanvabon* was a long way from home. The plates which showed every star of visual magnitude and could be stepped up to any desired magnification, portrayed stars of every imaginable degree of brilliance, in the startlingly different colours they show outside of atmosphere. But every one was unfamiliar. Only two constellations could be recognized as seen from Earth, and they were shrunken and distorted. The

Milky Way seemed vaguely out of place. But even such oddities were minor compared to a sight in the forward plates.

There was a vast, vast mistiness ahead. A luminous mist. It seemed motionless. It took a long time for any appreciable nearing to appear in the vision plates, though the spaceship's velocity indicator showed an incredible speed. The mist was the Crab Nebula, six light-years long, three and a half light-years thick, with outward-reaching members that in the telescopes of Earth gave it some resemblance to the creature for which it was named. It was a cloud of gas, infinitely tenuous, reaching half again as far as from Sol to its nearest neighbour-sun. Deep within it burned two stars; a double star; one component the familiar yellow of the sun of Earth, the other an unholy white.

Tommy Dort said meditatively:

'We're heading into a deep, sir?'

The skipper studied the last two plates of Tommy's taking, and put them aside. He went back to his uneasy contemplation of the vision plates ahead. The *Llanvabon* was decelerating at full force. She was a bare half light-year from the nebula. Tommy's work was guiding the ship's course, now, but the work was done. During all the stay of the exploring ship in the nebula, Tommy Dort would loaf. But he'd more than paid his way so far.

He had just completed a quite unique first – a complete photographic record of the movement of a nebula during a period of four thousand years, taken by one individual with the same apparatus and with control exposures to detect and record any systematic errors. It was an achievement in itself worth the journey from Earth. But in addition, he had also recorded four thousand years of the history of a double star, and four thousand years of the history of a star in the act of degenerating into a white dwarf.

It was not that Tommy Dort was four thousand years old. He was, actually, in his twenties. But the Crab Nebula is four thousand light-years from Earth, and the last two pictures had been taken by light which would not reach Earth until the sixth millennium AD. On the way here – at speeds incredible multiples of the speed of light – Tommy Dort had recorded each aspect of the nebula by the light which had left it from forty centuries since to a bare six months ago.

The *Llanvabon* bored on through space. Slowly, slowly, slowly, the incredible luminosity crept across the vision plates. It blotted out half the universe from view. Before was glowing mist, and behind was a star-studded emptiness. The mist shut off three-fourths of all the stars. Some few of the brightest shone dimly through it near its edge, but only a few. Then there was only an irregularly shaped patch of darkness astern against which stars shone unwinking. The *Llanvabon* dived into the nebula, and it seemed as if it bored into a tunnel of darkness with walls of shining fog.

Which was exactly what the spaceship was doing. The most distant photographs of all had disclosed structural features in the nebula. It was not amorphous. It had form. As the *Llanvabon* drew nearer, indications of structure grew more distinct, and Tommy Dort had argued for a curved approach for photographic reasons. So the spaceship had come up to the nebula on a vast logarithmic curve, and Tommy had been able to take successive photographs from slightly different angles and get stereopairs which showed the nebula in three dimensions; which disclosed billowings and hollows and an actually complicated shape. In places, the nebula displayed convolutions like those of a human brain. It was into one of those hollows that the spaceship now plunged. They had been called 'deeps' by analogy with crevasses on the ocean floor. And they promised to be useful.

The skipper relaxed. One of a skipper's functions, nowadays, is to think of things to worry about, and then worry about them. The skipper of the *Llanvabon* was conscientious. Only after a certain instrument remained definitely non-registering did he ease himself back in his seat.

'It was just barely possible,' he said heavily, 'that those deeps might be nonluminous gas. But they're empty. So we'll be able to use overdrive as long as we're in them.'

It was a light-year-and-a-half from the edge of the nebula to the neighbourhood of the double star which was its heart. That was the problem. A nebula is a gas. It is so thin that a comet's tail is solid by comparison, but a ship travelling on overdrive – above the speed of light – does not want to hit even a merely hard vacuum. It needs pure emptiness, such as exists between the stars. But the *Llanvabon* could not do much in this expanse of mist if it was limited to speeds a merely hard vacuum will permit.

The luminosity seemed to close in behind the spaceship, which slowed and slowed and slowed. The overdrive went off with the sudden *pinging* sensation which goes all over a person when the overdrive field is released.

Then, almost instantly, bells burst into clanging, strident uproar all through the ship. Tommy was almost deafened by the alarm bell which rang in the captain's room before the quartermaster shut it off with a flip of his hand. But other bells could be heard ringing throughout the rest of the ship, to be cut off as automatic doors closed one by one.

Tommy Dort stared at the skipper. The skipper's hands clenched. He was up and staring over the quartermaster's shoulder. One indicator was apparently having convulsions. Others strained to record their findings. A spot on the diffusedly bright mistiness of a bow-quartering visiplate grew brighter as the automatic scanner focused on it. That was the direction of the object which had sounded collision-alarm. But the object locator itself – . According to its reading, there was one solid object some eighty thousand miles away – an object of no great size. But there was another object whose distance varied from extreme range to zero, and whose size shared its impossible advance and retreat.

'Step up the scanner,' snapped the skipper.

The extra-bright spot on the scanner rolled outward, obliterating the undifferentiated image behind it. Magnification increased. But nothing appeared. Absolutely nothing. Yet the radio locator insisted that something monstrous and invisible made lunatic dashes towards the *Llanvabon*, at speeds which inevitably implied collision, and then fled coyly away at the same rate.

The visiplate went up to maximum magnification. Still nothing. The skipper ground his teeth. Tommy Dort said meditatively:

'D'you know, sir, I saw something like this on a liner on the Earth–Mars run once, when we were being located by another ship. Their locator beam was the same frequency as ours, and every time it hit, it registered like something monstrous, and solid.'

'That,' said the skipper savagely, 'is just what's happening now. There's something like a locator beam on us. We're getting that beam and our own echo besides. But the other ship's invisible! Who is out here in an invisible ship with locator devices? Not men, certainly!'

He pressed the button in his sleeve communicator and snapped:

'Action stations! Man all weapons! Condition of extreme alert in all departments immediately!'

His hands closed and unclosed. He stared again at the visiplate which showed nothing but a formless brightness.

'Not men?' Tommy Dort straightened sharply. 'You mean – '

'How many solar systems in our galaxy?' demanded the skipper bitterly. 'How many planets fit for life? And how many kinds of life could there be? If this ship isn't from Earth – and it isn't – it has a crew that isn't human. And things that aren't human but are up to the level of deep-space travel in their civilization could mean anything!'

The skipper's hands were actually shaking. He would not have talked so freely before a member of his own crew, but Tommy Dort was of the observation staff. And even a skipper whose duties include worrying may sometimes need desperately to unload his worries. Sometimes, too, it helps to think aloud.

'Something like this has been talked about and speculated about for years,' he said softly. 'Mathematically, it's been an odds-on bet that somewhere in our galaxy there'd be another race with a civilization equal to or further advanced than ours. Nobody could ever guess where or when we'd meet them. But it looks like we've done it now!'

Tommy's eyes were very bright.

'D'you suppose they'll be friendly, sir?'

The skipper glanced at the distance indicator. The phantom object still made its insane, nonexistent swoops towards and away from the *Llanvabon*. The secondary indication of an object at eighty thousand miles stirred ever so slightly.

'It's moving,' he said curtly. 'Heading for us. Just what we'd do if a strange spaceship appeared in our hunting grounds! Friendly? Maybe! We're going to try to contact them. We have to. But I suspect this is the end of this expedition. Thank God for the blasters!'

The blasters are those beams of ravening destruction which take care of recalcitrant meteorites in a spaceship's course when the deflectors can't handle them. They are not designed as weapons, but they can serve as pretty good ones. They can go into action at five thousand miles, and draw on the entire power output of a whole ship. With automatic aim and a traverse of five degrees, a ship like the *Llanvabon* can come very close to blasting a hole through a small-sized asteroid which gets in its way. But not on overdrive, of course.

Tommy Dort had approached the bow-quartering visiplate. Now he jerked his head around.

'Blasters sir? What for?'

The skipper grimaced at the empty visiplate.

'Because we don't know what they're like and can't take a chance! I know!' he added bitterly. 'We're going to make contact and try to find out all we can about them – especially where they come from. I suppose we'll try to make friends – but we haven't much chance. We can't trust them the fraction of an inch. We daren't! They've locators. Maybe they've tracers better than any we have. Maybe they could trace us all the way home without our knowing it! We can't risk a nonhuman race knowing where Earth is unless we're sure of them! And how can we be sure? They could come to trade, of course – or they could swoop down on overdrive with a battle fleet that could wipe us out before we knew what happened. We wouldn't know which to expect, or when!'

Tommy's face was startled.

'It's all been thrashed out over and over, in theory,' said the skipper. 'Nobody's ever been able to find a sound answer, even on paper. But you know, in all their theorizing, no one considered the crazy, rank impossibility of a deep-space contact, with neither side knowing the other's home world! But we've got to find an answer in fact! What are we going to do about them? Maybe these creatures will be aesthetic marvels, nice and friendly and polite – and underneath with the sneaking brutal ferocity of a Japanese. Or maybe they'll be crude and gruff as a Swedish farmer – and just as decent underneath. Maybe they're something in between. But am I going to risk the possible future of the human race on a guess that it's safe to trust them? God knows it would be worth while to make friends with a new civilization! It would be bound to stimulate our own, and maybe we'd gain enormously. But I can't take chances. The one thing I won't risk is having them know how to find Earth! Either I know they can't follow me, or I don't go home! And they'll probably feel the same way!'

He pressed the sleeve-communicator button again.

'Navigation officers, attention! Every star map on this ship is to be prepared for instant destruction. This includes photographs and diagrams from which our course or starting point could be deduced. I want all astronomical data gathered and arranged to be destroyed in a split second, on order. Make it fast and report when ready!'

He released the button. He looked suddenly old. The first contact of humanity with an alien race was a situation which had been foreseen in many fashions, but never one quite so hopeless of solution as this. A solitary Earth-ship and a solitary alien, meeting in a nebula which must be remote from the home planet of each. They might wish peace, but the line of conduct which best prepared a treacherous attack was just the seeming of friendliness. Failure to be suspicious might doom the human race – and a peaceful exchange of the fruits of civilization would be the greatest benefit imaginable. Any mistake would be irreparable, but a failure to be on guard would be fatal.

The captain's room was very, very quiet. The bow-quartering visiplate was filled with the image of a very small section of the nebula. A very small section indeed. It was all diffused, featureless, luminous mist. But suddenly Tommy Dort pointed.

'There, sir!'

There was a small shape in the mist. It was far away. It was a black shape, not polished to mirror-reflection like the hull of the *Llanvabon*. It was bulbous – roughly pear-shaped. There was much thin luminosity between, and no details could be observed, but it was surely no natural object. Then Tommy looked at the distance indicator and said quietly:

'It's headed for us at very high acceleration, sir. The odds are that they're thinking the same thing, sir, that neither of us will dare let the other go home. Do you think they'll try a contact with us, or let loose with their weapons as soon as they're in range?'

The *Llanvabon* was no longer in a crevasse of emptiness in the nebula's thin substance. She swam in luminescence. There were no stars save the two fierce glows in the nebula's heart. There was nothing but an all-enveloping light, curiously like one's imagining of underwater in the tropics of Earth.

The alien ship had made one sign of less than lethal intention. As it drew near the *Llanvabon*, it decelerated. The *Llanvabon* itself had advanced for a meeting and then come to a dead stop. Its movement had been a recognition of the nearness of the other ship. Its pausing was both a friendly sign and a precaution against attack. Relatively still, it could swivel on its own axis to present the least target to a slashing assault, and it would have a longer firing-time than if the two ships flashed past each other at their combined speeds.

The moment of actual approach, however, was tenseness

itself. The *Llanvabon*'s needle-pointed bow aimed unwaveringly at the alien bulk. A relay to the captain's room put a key under his hand which would fire the blasters with maximum power. Tommy Dort watched, his brow wrinkled. The aliens must be of a high degree of civilization if they had spaceships, and civilization does not develop without the development of foresight. These aliens must recognize all the implications of this first contact of two civilized races as fully as did the humans on the *Llanvabon.*

The possibility of an enormous spurt in the development of both, by peaceful contact and exchange of their separate technologies, would probably appeal to them as to the man. But when dissimilar human cultures are in contact, one must usually be subordinate or there is war. But subordination between races arising on separate planets could not be peacefully arranged. Men, at least, would never consent to subordination, nor was it likely that any highly-developed race would agree. The benefits to be derived from commerce could never make up for a condition of inferiority. Some races – men, perhaps – would prefer commerce to conquest. Perhaps – perhaps! – these aliens would also. But some types even of human beings would have craved red war. If the alien ship now approaching the *Llanvabon* returned to its home base with news of humanity's existence and of ships like the *Llanvabon,* it would give its race the choice of trade or battle. They might want trade, or they might want war. But it takes two to make trade, and only one to make war. They could not be sure of men's peacefulness, nor could men be sure of theirs. The only safety for either civilization would lie in the destruction of one or both of the two ships here and now.

But even victory would not be really enough. Men would need to know where this alien race was to be found, for avoidance if not for battle. They would need to know its weapons, and its resources, and if it could be a menace and how it could be eliminated in case of need. The aliens would feel the same necessities concerning humanity.

So the skipper of the *Llanvabon* did not press the key

which might possibly have blasted the other ship to nothingness. He dared not. But he dare not not fire either. Sweat came out on his face.

A speaker muttered. Someone from the range room.

'The other ship's stopped, sir. Quite stationary. Blasters are centred on it, sir.'

It was an urging to fire. But the skipper shook his head, to himself. The alien ship was no more than twenty miles away. It was dead-black. Every bit of its exterior was an abysmal, nonreflecting sable. No details could be seen except by minor variations in its outline against the misty nebula.

'It's stopped dead, sir,' said another voice. 'They've sent a modulated short wave at us, sir. Frequency modulated. Apparently a signal. Not enough power to do any harm.'

The skipper said through tight-locked teeth:

'They're doing something now. There's movement on the outside of their hull. Watch what comes out. Put the auxiliary blasters on it.'

Something small and round came smoothly out of the oval outline of the black ship. The bulbous hulk moved.

'Moving away, sir,' said the speaker. 'The object they let out is stationary in the place they've left.'

Another voice cut in:

'More frequency modulated stuff, sir. Unintelligible.'

Tommy Dort's eyes brightened. The skipper watched the visiplate, with sweat-droplets on his forehead.

'Rather pretty, sir,' said Tommy, meditatively. 'If they sent anything towards us, it might seem a projectile or a bomb. So they came close, let out a lifeboat, and went away again. They figure we can send a boat or a man to make contact without risking our ship. They must think pretty much as we do.'

The skipper said, without moving his eyes from the plate:

'Mr Dort, would you care to go out and look the thing over? I can't order you, but I need all my operating crew for emergencies. The observation staff – '

'Is expendable. Very well, sir,' said Tommy briskly. 'I won't take a lifeboat, sir. Just a suit with a drive in it. It's smaller and the arms and legs will look unsuitable for a bomb. I think I should carry a scanner, sir.'

The alien ship continued to retreat. Forty, eighty, four hundred miles. It came to a stop and hung there, waiting. Climbing into his atomic-driven spacesuit just within the *Llanvabon*'s air lock, Tommy heard the reports as they went over the speakers throughout the ship. That the other ship had stopped its retreat at four hundred miles was encouraging. It might not have weapons effective at a greater distance than that, and so felt safe. But just as the thought formed itself in his mind, the alien retreated precipitately still farther. Which, as Tommy reflected as he emerged from the lock, might be because the aliens had realized they were giving themselves away, or might be because they wanted to give the impression that they had done so.

He swooped away from the silvery-mirror *Llanvabon*, through a brightly glowing emptiness which was past any previous experience of the human race. Behind him, the *Llanvabon* swung about and darted away. The skipper's voice came in Tommy's helmet phones.

'We're pulling back, too, Mr Dort. There is a bare possibility that they've some explosive atomic reaction they can't use from their own ship, but which might be destructive even as far as this. We'll draw back. Keep your scanner on the object.'

The reasoning was sound, if not very comforting. An explosive which would destroy anything within twenty miles was theoretically possible, but humans didn't have it yet. It was decidedly safest for the *Llanvabon* to draw back.

But Tommy Dort felt very lonely. He sped through emptiness towards the tiny black speck which hung in incredible brightness. The *Llanvabon* vanished. Its polished hull would merge with the glowing mist at a relatively short distance, anyhow. The alien ship was not visible to the naked eye, either.

Tommy swam in nothingness, four thousand light-years from home, towards a tiny black spot which was the only solid object to be seen in all of space.

It was a slightly distorted sphere, not much over six feet in diameter. It bounced away when Tommy landed on it, feet-first. There were small tentacles, or horns, which projected in every direction. They looked rather like the detonating horns of a submarine mine, but there was a glint of crystal at the tip-end of each.

'I'm here,' said Tommy into his helmet phone.

He caught hold of a horn and drew himself to the object. It was all metal, dead-black. He could feel no texture through his space gloves, of course, but he went over and over it, trying to discover its purpose.

'Deadlock, sir,' he said presently. 'Nothing to report that the scanner hasn't shown you.'

Then, through his suit, he felt vibrations. They translated themselves as clankings. A section of the rounded hull of the object opened out. Two sections. He worked his way around to look in and see the first nonhuman civilized beings that any man had ever looked upon.

But what he saw was simply a flat plate on which dim-red glows crawled here and there in seeming aimlessness. His helmet phones emitted a startled exclamation. The skipper's voice:

'Very good, Mr Dort. Fix your scanner to look into that plate. They dumped out a robot with an infrared visiplate for communication. Not risking any personnel. Whatever we might do would damage only machinery. Maybe they expect us to bring it on board – and it may have a bomb charge that can be detonated when they're ready to start for home. I'll send a plate to face one of its scanners. You return to the ship.'

'Yes, sir,' said Tommy. 'But which way is the ship, sir?'

There were no stars. The nebula obscured them with its light. The only thing visible from the robot was the double star at the nebula's centre. Tommy was no longer oriented. He had but one reference point.

'Head straight away from the double star,' came the order in his helmet phone. 'We'll pick you up.'

He passed another lonely figure, a little later, headed for the alien sphere with a vision plate to set up. The two spaceships, each knowing that it dared not risk its own race by the slightest lack of caution, would communicate with each other through this small round robot. Their separate vision systems would enable them to exchange all the information they dared give, while they debated the most practical way of making sure that their own civilization would not be endangered by this first contact with another. The truly most practical method would be the destruction of the other ship in a swift and deadly attack – in self-defence.

II

The *Llanvabon*, thereafter, was a ship in which there were two separate enterprises on hand at the same time. She had come out from Earth to make close-range observations on the smaller component of the double star at the nebula's centre. The nebula itself was the result of the most titanic explosion of which men have any knowledge. The explosion took place some time in the year 2946 BC, before the first of the seven cities of long-dead Illium was even thought of. The light of that explosion reached Earth in the year AD 1054, and was duly recorded in ecclesiastic annals and somewhat more reliably by Chinese court astronomers. It was bright enough to be seen in daylight for twenty-three successive days. Its light – and it was four thousand light-years away – was brighter than that of Venus.

From these facts, astronomers could calculate nine hundred years later the violence of the detonation. Matter blown away from the centre of the explosion would have travelled outwards at the rate of two million three hundred thousand miles an hour; more than thirty-eight thousand miles a minute; something over six hundred and thirty-eight miles per second. When twentieth-century telescopes were turned upon the scene of this vast explosion, only a double star remained –

and the nebula. The brighter star of the doublet was almost unique in having so high a surface temperature that it showed no spectrum lines at all. It had a continuous spectrum. Sol's surface temperature is about 7000° Absolute. That of the hot white star is 500,000 degrees. It has nearly the mass of the sun, but only one-fifth its diameter, so that its density is one hundred and seventy-three times that of water, sixteen times that of lead, and eight times that of iridium – the heaviest substance known on Earth. But even this density is not that of a dwarf white star like the companion of Sirius. The white star in the Crab Nebula is an incomplete dwarf; it is a star still in the act of collapsing. Examination – including the survey of a four-thousand-year column of its light – was worth while. The *Llanvabon* had come to make that examination. But the finding of an alien spaceship upon a similar errand had implications which overshadowed the original purpose of the expedition.

A tiny bulbous robot floated in the tenuous nebular gas. The normal operating crew of the *Llanvabon* stood at their posts with a sharp alertness which was productive of tense nerves. The observation staff divided itself, and a part went half-heartedly about the making of the observations for which the *Llanvabon* had come. The other half applied itself to the problem the spaceship offered.

It represented a culture which was up to space travel on an interstellar scale. The explosion of a mere five thousand years since must have blasted every trace of life out of existence in the area now filled by the nebula. So the aliens of the black spaceship came from another solar system. Their trip must have been, like that of the Earth ship, for purely scientific purposes. There was nothing to be extracted from the nebula.

They were, then, at least near the level of human civilization, which meant that they had or could develop arts and articles of commerce which men would want to trade for, in friendship. But they would necessarily realize that the existence and civilization of humanity was a potential menace to their own race. The two races could be friends, but also they could be deadly enemies. Each, even if unwillingly, was a monstrous menace to the other. And the only safe thing to do with a menace is to destroy it.

In the Crab Nebula the problem was acute and immediate. The future relationship of the two races would be settled here and now. If a process for friendship could be established, one race, otherwise doomed, would survive and both would benefit immensely. But that process had to be established, and confidence built up, without the most minute risk of danger from treachery. Confidence would need to be established upon a foundation of necessarily complete distrust. Neither dared return to its own base if the other could do harm to its race. Neither dared risk any of the necessities to trust. The only safe thing for either to do was destroy the other or be destroyed.

But even for war, more was needed than mere destruction of the other. With interstellar traffic, the aliens must have atomic power and some form of overdrive for travel above the speed of light. With radio location and visiplates and short-wave communication they had, of course, many other devices. What weapons did they have? How widely extended was their culture? What were their resources? Could there be a development of trade and friendship, or were the two races so unlike that only war could exist between them? If peace was possible, how could it be begun?

The men on the *Llanvabon* needed facts – and so did the crew of the other ship. They must take back every morsel of information they could. The most important information of all would be of the location of the other civilization, just in case of war. That one bit of information might be the decisive factor in an interstellar war. But other facts would be enormously valuable.

The tragic thing was that there could be no possible information which could lead to peace. Neither ship could stake its own race's existence upon any conviction of the goodwill or the honour of the other.

So there was a strange truce between the two ships. The alien went about its work of making observations, as did the

Llanvabon. The tiny robot floated in bright emptiness. A scanner from the *Llanvabon* was focused upon a vision plate from the alien. A scanner from the alien regarded a vision plate from the *Llanvabon.* Communication began.

It progressed rapidly. Tommy Dort was one of those who made the first progress report. His special task on the expedition was over. He had now been assigned to work on the problem of communication with the alien entities. He went with the ship's solitary psychologist to the captain's room to convey the news of success. The captain's room, as usual, was a place of silence and dull-red indicator lights and the great bright visiplates on every wall and on the ceiling.

'We've established fairly satisfactory communication, sir,' said the psychologist. He looked tired. His work on the trip was supposed to be that of measuring personal factors of error in the observation staff, for the reduction of all observations to the nearest possible decimal to the absolute. He had been pressed into service for which he was not especially fitted, and it told upon him. 'That is, we can say almost anything we wish to them, and can understand what they say in return. But of course we don't know how much of what they say is the truth.'

The skipper's eyes turned to Tommy Dort.

'We've hooked up some machinery,' said Tommy, 'that amounts to a mechanical translator. We have vision plates, of course, and then short-wave beams direct. They use frequency-modulation plus what is probably variation in wave forms – like our vowel and consonant sounds in speech. We've never had any use for anything like that before, so our coils won't handle it, but we've developed a sort of code which isn't the language of either set of us. They shoot over short-wave stuff with frequency-modulation, and we record it as sound. When we shoot it back, it's reconverted into frequency-modulation.'

The skipper said, frowning:

'Why wave-form changes in short waves? How do you know?'

'We showed them our recorder in the vision plates, and they showed us theirs. They record the frequency-modulation direct. I think,' said Tommy carefully, 'they don't use sound at all, even in speech. They've set up a communications room, and we've watched them in the act of communicating with us. They make no perceptible movement of anything that corresponds to a speech organ. Instead of a microphone, they simply stand near something that would work as a pick-up antenna. My guess, sir, is that they use microwaves for what you might call person-to-person conversation. I think they make short-wave trains as we make sounds.'

The skipper stared at him:

'That means they have telepathy?'

'M-m-m. Yes, sir,' said Tommy. 'Also it means that we have telepathy too, as far as they are concerned. They're probably deaf. They've certainly no idea of using sound waves in air for communication. They simply don't use noises for any purpose.'

The skipper stored the information away.

'What else?'

'Well, sir,' said Tommy doubtfully, 'I think we're all set. We agreed on arbitrary symbols for objects, sir, by way of the visiplates, and worked out relationships and verbs and so on with diagrams and pictures. We've a couple of thousand words that have mutual meanings. We set up an analyser to sort out their short-wave groups, which we feed into a decoding machine. And then the coding end of the machine picks out recordings to make the wave groups we want to send back. When you're ready to talk to the skipper of the other ship, sir, I think we're ready.'

'H-m-m. What's your impression of their psychology?' The skipper asked the question of the psychologist.

'I don't know, sir,' said the psychologist harassedly. 'They seem to be completely direct. But they haven't let slip even a hint of the tenseness we know exists. They act as if they were simply setting up a means of communication for friendly conversation. But there is . . . well . . . an overtone – '

The psychologist was a good man at psychological mensuration, which is a good and useful field. But he was not equipped to analyse a completely alien thought-pattern.

'If I may say so, sir – ' said Tommy uncomfortably.

'What?'

'They're oxygen breathers,' said Tommy, 'and they're not too dissimilar to us in other ways. It seems to me, sir, that paralleled evolution has been at work. Perhaps intelligence evolves in parallel lines, just as . . . well . . . basic bodily functions. I mean,' he added conscientiously, 'any living being of any sort must ingest, metabolize, and excrete. Perhaps any intelligent brain must perceive, apperceive, and find a personal reaction. I'm sure I've detected irony. That implies humour, too. In short, sir, I think they could be likeable.'

The skipper heaved himself to his feet.

'H-m-m,' he said profoundly. 'We'll see what they have to say.'

He walked to the communications room. The scanner for the vision plate in the robot was in readiness. The skipper walked in front of it. Tommy Dort sat down at the coding machine and tapped at the keys. Highly improbable noises came from it, went into a microphone, and governed the frequency-modulation of a signal sent through space to the other spaceship. Almost instantly the vision screen which with one relay – in the robot – showed the interior of the other ship lighted up. An alien came before the scanner and seemed to look inquisitively out of the plate. He was extraordinarily manlike, but he was not human. The impression he gave was of extreme baldness and a somehow humorous frankness.

'I'd like to say,' said the skipper heavily, 'the appropriate things about this first contact of two dissimilar civilized races, and of my hopes that a friendly intercourse between the two peoples will result.'

Tommy Dort hesitated. Then he shrugged and tapped expertly upon the coder. More improbable noises.

The alien skipper seemed to receive the message. He made a

gesture which was wryly assenting. The decoder on the *Llanvabon* hummed to itself and word-cards dropped into the message frame. Tommy said dispassionately:

'He says, sir, "That is all very well, but is there any way for us to let each other go home alive? I would be happy to hear of such a way if you can contrive one. At the moment it seems to me that one of us must be killed." '

III

The atmosphere was of confusion. There were too many questions to be answered all at once. Nobody could answer any of them. And all of them had to be answered.

The *Llanvabon* could start for home. The alien ship might or might not be able to multiply the speed of light by one more unit than the Earth vessel. If it could, the *Llanvabon* would get close enough to Earth to reveal its destination – and then have to fight. It might or might not win. Even if it did win, the aliens might have a communication system by which the *Llanvabon*'s destination might have been reported to the aliens' home planet before battle was joined. But the *Llanvabon* might lose in such a fight. If she was to be destroyed, it would be better to be destroyed here, without giving any clue to where human beings might be found by a forewarned, fore-armed alien battle fleet.

The black ship was in exactly the same predicament. It, too, could start for home. But the *Llanvabon* might be faster, and an overdrive field can be trailed, if you set to work on it soon enough. The aliens, also, would not know whether the *Llanvabon* could report to its home base without returning. If the alien was to be destroyed, it also would prefer to fight it out here, so that it could not lead a probable enemy to its own civilization.

Neither ship, then, could think of flight. The course of the *Llanvabon* into the nebula might be known to the black ship, but it had been the end of a logarithmic curve, and the aliens could not know its properties. They could not tell from that from what direction the Earth ship had started. As of the moment, then, the two ships were even. But the question was and remained, 'What now?'

There was no specific answer. The aliens traded information for information – and did not always realize what information they gave. The humans traded information for information – and Tommy Dort sweated blood in his anxiety not to give any clue to the whereabouts of Earth.

The aliens saw by infrared light, and the vision plates and scanners in the robot communication-exchange had to adapt their respective images up and down an optical octave each, for them to have any meaning at all. It did not occur to the aliens that their eyesight told that their sun was a red dwarf, yielding light of greatest energy just below the part of the spectrum visible to human eyes. But after that fact was realized on the *Llanvabon*, it was realized that the aliens, also, should be able to deduce the Sun's spectral type by the light to which men's eyes were best adapted.

There was a gadget for the recording of short-wave trains which was so casually in use among the aliens as a sound-recorder is among men. The humans wanted that, badly. And the aliens were fascinated by the mystery of sound. They were able to perceive noise, of course, just as a man's palm will perceive infrared light by the sensation of heat it produces, but they could no more differentiate pitch or tone-quality than a man is able to distinguish between two frequencies of heat-radiation even half an octave apart. To them, the human science of sound was a remarkable discovery. They would find uses for noises which humans had never imagined – if they lived.

But that was another question. Neither ship could leave without first destroying the other. But while the flood of information was in passage, neither ship could afford to destroy the other. There was the matter of the outer colouring of the two ships. The *Llanvabon* was mirror-bright exteriorly. The alien ship was dead-black by visible light. It absorbed heat to perfection, and should radiate it away again as readily. But it did not. The black coating was not a 'black body' colour or lack of colour. It was a perfect reflector of certain infrared wave lengths while simultaneously it fluoresced in just those wave bands. In practice, it absorbed the higher frequencies of heat, converted them to lower frequencies it did not radiate – and stayed at the desired temperature even in empty space.

Tommy Dort laboured over his task of communications. He found the alien thought-processes not so alien that he could not follow them. The discussion of techniques reached the matter of interstellar navigation. A star map was needed to illustrate the process. It would not have been logical to use a star map from the chart room – but from a star map one could guess the point from which the map was projected. Tommy had a map made specially, with imaginary but convincing star images upon it. He translated directions for its use by the coder and decoder. In return, the aliens presented a star map of their own before the visiplate. Copied instantly by photograph, the Nav officers laboured over it, trying to figure out from what spot in the galaxy the stars and Milky Way would show at such an angle. It baffled them.

It was Tommy who realized finally that the aliens had made a special star map for their demonstration too, and that it was a mirror-image of the faked map Tommy had shown them previously.

Tommy could grin, at that. He began to like these aliens. They were not human, but they had a very human sense of the ridiculous. In course of time Tommy essayed a mild joke. It had to be translated into code numerals, these into quite cryptic groups of short-wave, frequency-modulated impulses, and these went to the other ship and into heaven knew what to become intelligible. A joke which went through such formalities would not seem likely to be funny. But the aliens did see the point.

There was one of the aliens to whom communication became as normal a function as Tommy's own code-handlings. The two of them developed a quite insane friendship, conversing by coder, decoder, and short-wave trains. When technicalities in the official messages grew too involved, that alien sometimes threw in strictly nontechnical interpolations akin to slang. Often they cleared up the confusion. Tommy, for no reason whatever, had filed a code-name of 'Buck' which the decoder picked out regularly when this particular alien signed his own symbol to a message.

In the third week of communication, the decoder suddenly presented Tommy with a message in the message frame.

You are a good guy. It is too bad we have to kill each other. – Buck.

Tommy had been thinking much the same thing. He tapped off the rueful reply:

We can't see any way out of it. Can you?

There was a pause, and the message frame filled up again.

If we could believe each other, yes. Our skipper would like it. But we can't believe you, and you can't believe us. We'd trail you home if we got a chance, and you'd trail us. But we feel sorry about it. – Buck.

Tommy Dort took the messages to the skipper.

'Look here, sir!' he said urgently. 'These people are almost human, and they're likeable cusses.'

The skipper was busy about his important task of thinking of things to worry about, and worrying about them. He said tiredly:

'They're oxygen breathers. Their air is twenty-eight per cent oxygen instead of twenty, but they could do very well on Earth. It would be a highly desirable conquest for them. And we still don't know what weapons they've got or what they can develop. Would you tell them how to find Earth?'

'N-no,' said Tommy, unhappily.

'They probably feel the same way,' said the skipper dryly. 'And if we did manage to make a friendly contact, how long would it stay friendly? If their weapons were inferior to ours, they'd feel that for their own safety they had to improve them.

And we, knowing they were planning to revolt, would crush them while we could – for our own safety! If it happened to be the other way about, they'd have to smash us before we could catch up to them.'

Tommy was silent, but he moved restlessly.

'If we smash this black ship and get home,' said the skipper, 'Earth Government will be annoyed if we don't tell them where it came from. But what can we do? We'll be lucky enough to get back alive with our warning. It isn't possible to get out of those creatures any more information than we give them, and we surely won't give them our address! We've run into them by accident. Maybe – if we smash this ship – there won't be another contact for thousands of years. And it's a pity, because trade could mean so much! But it takes two to make a peace, and we can't risk trusting them. The only answer is to kill them if we can, and if we can't, to make sure that when they kill us they'll find out nothing that will lead them to Earth. I don't like it,' added the skipper tiredly, 'but there simply isn't anything else to do!'

IV

On the *Llanvabon*, the technicians worked frantically in two divisions. One prepared for victory, and the other for defeat. The ones working for victory could do little. The main blasters were the only weapons with any promise. Their mountings were cautiously altered so that they were no longer fixed nearly dead ahead, with only a 5° traverse. Electronic controls which followed a radio-locator master-finder would keep them trained with absolute precision upon a given target regardless of its manoeuvrings. More: a hitherto unsung genius in the engine room devised a capacity-storage system by which the normal full-output of the ship's engines could be momentarily accumulated and released in surges of stored power far above normal. In theory, the range of the blasters should be multiplied and their destructive power considerably stepped up. But there was not much more that could be done.

The defeat crew had more leeway. Star charts, navigational

instruments carrying telltale notations, the photographic record Tommy Dort had made on the six-months' journey from Earth, and every other memorandum offering clues to Earth's position, were prepared for destruction. They were put in sealed files, and if any one of them was opened by one who did not know the exact, complicated process, the contents of all the files would flash into ashes and the ash be churned past any hope of restoration. Of course, if the *Llanvabon* should be victorious, a carefully not-indicated method of reopening them in safety would remain.

There were atomic bombs placed all over the hull of the ship. If its human crew should be killed without complete destruction of the ship, the atomic-power bombs should detonate if the *Llanvabon* was brought alongside the alien vessel. There were no ready-made atomic bombs on board, but there were small spare atomic-power units on board. It was not hard to trick them so that when they were turned on, instead of yielding a smooth flow of power they would explode. And four men of the Earth ship's crew remained always in spacesuits with closed helmets, to right the ship should it be punctured in many compartments by an unwarned attack.

Such an attack, however, would not be treacherous. The alien skipper had spoken frankly. His manner was that of one who wryly admits the uselessness of lies. The skipper and the *Llanvabon*, in turn, heavily admitted the virtue of frankness. Each insisted – perhaps truthfully – that he wished for friendship between the two races. But neither could trust the other not to make every conceivable effort to find out the one thing he needed most desperately to conceal – the location of his home planet. And neither dared believe that the other was unable to trail him and find out. Because each felt it his own duty to accomplish that unbearable – to the other – act, neither could risk the possible existence of his race by trusting the other. They must fight because they could not do anything else.

They could raise the stakes of the battle by an exchange of information beforehand. But there was a limit to the stake either would put up. No information on weapons, population, or resources would be given by either. Not even the distance of their home bases from the Crab Nebula would be told. They exchanged information, to be sure, but they knew a battle to the death must follow, and each strove to represent his own civilization as powerful enough to give pause to the other's ideas of possible conquest – and thereby increased its appearance of menace to the other, and made battle more unavoidable.

It was curious how completely such alien brains could mesh, however. Tommy Dort, sweating over the coding and decoding machines, found a personal equation emerging from the at first stilted arrays of word-cards which arranged themselves. He had seen the aliens only in the vision screen, and then only in light at least one octave removed from the light they saw by. They, in turn, saw him very strangely, by transposed illumination from what to them would be the far ultraviolet. But their brains worked alike. Amazingly alike. Tommy Dort felt an actual sympathy and even something close to friendship for the gill-breathing, bald, and dryly ironic creatures of the black space vessel.

Because of that mental kinship he set up – though hopelessly – a sort of table of the aspects of the problem before them. He did not believe that the aliens had any instinctive desire to destroy man. In fact, the study of communications from the aliens had produced on the *Llanvabon* a feeling of tolerance not unlike that between enemy soldiers during a truce on Earth. The men felt no enmity, and probably neither did the aliens. But they had to kill or be killed for strictly logical reasons.

Tommy's table was specific. He made a list of objectives the men must try to achieve, in the order of their importance. The first was the carrying back of news of the existence of the alien culture. The second was the location of that alien culture in the galaxy. The third was the carrying back of as much information as possible about that culture. The third was being worked on, but the second was probably impossible. The first – and all – would depend on the result of the fight which must take place.

The aliens' objectives would be exactly similar, so that the men must prevent, first, news of the existence of Earth's culture from being taken back by the aliens, second, alien discovery of the location of Earth, and third, the acquiring by the aliens of information which would help them or encourage them to attack humanity. And again the third was in train, and the second was probably taken care of, and the first must await the battle.

There was no possible way to avoid the grim necessity of the destruction of the black ship. The aliens would see no solution to their problems but the destruction of the *Llanvabon*. But Tommy Dort, regarding his tabulation ruefully, realized that even complete victory would not be a perfect solution. The ideal would be for the *Llanvabon* to take back the alien ship for study. Nothing less would be a complete attainment of the third objective. But Tommy realized that he hated the idea of so complete a victory, even if it could be accomplished. He would hate the idea of killing even nonhuman creatures who understood a human joke. And beyond that, he would hate the idea of Earth fitting out a fleet of fighting ships to destroy an alien culture because its existence was dangerous. The pure accident of this encounter, between peoples who could like each other, had created a situation which could only result in wholesale destruction.

Tommy Dort soured on his own brain which could find no answer which would work. But there had to be an answer! The gamble was too big! It was too absurd that two spaceships should fight – neither one primarily designed for fighting – so that the survivor could carry back news which would set one race to frenzied preparation for war against the unwarned other.

If both races could be warned, though, and each knew that the other did not want to fight, and if they could communicate with each other but not locate each other until some grounds for mutual trust could be reached –

It was impossible. It was chimerical. It was a daydream. It was nonsense. But it was such luring nonsense that Tommy Dort ruefully put it into the coder to his gill-breathing friend Buck, then some hundred thousand miles off in the misty brightness of the nebula.

'Sure,' said Buck, in the decoder's word-cards flicking into place in the message frame. 'That is a good dream. But I like you and still won't believe you. If I said that first, you would like me but not believe me either. I tell you the truth more than you believe, and maybe you tell me the truth more than I believe. But there is no way to know. I am sorry.'

Tommy Dort stared gloomily at the message. He felt a very horrible sense of responsibility. Everyone did, on the *Llanvabon*. If they failed in this encounter, the human race would run a very good chance of being exterminated in time to come. If they succeeded, the race of the aliens would be the one to face destruction, most likely. Millions or billions of lives hung upon the actions of a few men.

Then Tommy Dort saw the answer.

It would be amazingly simple, if it worked. At worst it might give a partial victory to humanity and the *Llanvabon*. He sat quite still, not daring to move lest he break the chain of thought that followed the first tenuous idea. He went over and over it, excitedly finding objections here and meeting them, and overcoming impossibilities there. It was the answer! He felt sure of it.

He felt almost dizzy with relief when he found his way to the captain's room and asked leave to speak.

It is the function of a skipper, among others, to find things to worry about. But the *Llanvabon*'s skipper did not have to look. In the three weeks and four days since the first contact with the alien black ship, the skipper's face had grown lined and old. He had not only the *Llanvabon* to worry about. He had all of humanity.

'Sir,' said Tommy Dort, his mouth rather dry because of his

enormous earnestness, 'may I offer a method of attack on the black ship? I'll undertake it myself, sir, and if it doesn't work our ship won't be weakened.'

The skipper looked at him unseeingly.

'The tactics are all worked out, Mr Dort,' he said heavily. 'They're being cut on tape now, for the ship's handling. It's a terrible gamble, but it has to be done.'

'I think,' said Tommy carefully, 'I've worked out a way to take the gamble out. Suppose, sir, we send a message to the other ship, offering – '

His voice went on in the utterly quiet captain's room, with the visiplates showing only a vast mistiness outside and the two fiercely burning stars in the nebula's heart.

V

The skipper himself went through the air lock with Tommy. For one reason, the action Tommy had suggested would need his authority behind it. For another, the skipper had worried more intensively than anybody else on the *Llanvabon*, and he was tired of it. If he went with Tommy, he would do the thing himself, and if he failed he would be the first one killed – and the tape for the Earth ship's manoeuvring was already fed into the control board and correlated with the master-timer. If Tommy and the skipper were killed, a single control pushed home would throw the *Llanvabon* into the most furious possible all-out attack, which would end in the complete destruction of one ship or the other – or both. So the skipper was not deserting his post.

The outer air lock door swung wide. It opened upon that shining emptiness which was the nebula. Twenty miles away, the little round robot hung in space, drifting in an incredible orbit about the twin central suns, and floating ever nearer and nearer. It would never reach either of them, of course. The white star alone was so much hotter than Earth's sun that its heat-effect would produce Earth's temperature on an object five times as far from it as Neptune is from Sol. Even removed to the distance of Pluto, the little robot would be raised to cherry-red heat by the blazing white dwarf. And it could not possibly approach to the ninety-odd million miles which is the Earth's distance from the sun. So near, its metal would melt and boil away as vapour. But, half a light-year out, the bulbous object bobbed in emptiness.

The two spacesuited figures soared away from the *Llanvabon*. The small atomic drives which made them minute spaceships on their own had been subtly altered, but the change did not interfere with their functioning. They headed for the communication robot. The skipper, out in space, said gruffly:

'Mr Dort, all my life I have longed for adventure. This is the first time I could ever justify it to myself.'

His voice came through Tommy's space-phone receivers. Tommy wetted his lips and said:

'It doesn't seem like adventure to me, sir. I want terribly for the plan to go through. I thought adventure was when you didn't care.'

'Oh, no,' said the skipper. 'Adventure is when you toss your life on the scales of chance and wait for the pointer to stop.'

They reached the round object. They clung to its short, scanner-tipped horns.

'Intelligent, those creatures,' said the skipper heavily. 'They must want desperately to see more of our ship than the communications room, to agree to this exchange of visits before the fight.'

'Yes, sir,' said Tommy. But privately, he suspected that Buck – his gill-breathing friend – would like to see him in the flesh before one or both of them died. And it seemed to him that between the two ships had grown up an odd tradition of courtesy, like that between two ancient knights before a journey, when they admired each other wholeheartedly before hacking at each other with all the contents of their respective armouries.

They waited.

Then, out of the mist, came two other figures. The alien spacesuits were also power-driven. The aliens themselves were shorter than men, and their helmet openings were coated with a filtering material to cut off visible and ultraviolet rays which to them would be lethal. It was not possible to see more than the outline of the heads within.

Tommy's helmet phone said, from the communications room on the *Llanvabon*:

'They say that their ship is waiting for you, sir. The air lock door will be open.'

The skipper's voice said heavily:

'Mr Dort, have you seen their spacesuits before? If so, are you sure they're not carrying anything extra, such as bombs?'

'Yes, sir,' said Tommy. 'We've shown each other our space equipment. They've nothing but regular stuff in view, sir.'

The skipper made a gesture to the two aliens. He and Tommy Dort plunged on for the black vessel. They could not make out the ship very clearly with the naked eye, but directions for change of course came from the communications room.

The black ship loomed up. It was huge; as long as the *Llanvabon* and vastly thicker. The air lock did stand open. The two spacesuited men moved in and anchored themselves with magnetic-soled boots. The outer door closed. There was a rush of air and simultaneously the sharp quick tug of artificial gravity. Then the inner door opened.

All was darkness. Tommy switched on his helmet light at the same instant as the skipper. Since the aliens saw by infra-red, a white light would have been intolerable to them. The men's helmet lights were, therefore, of the deep-red tint used to illuminate instrument panels so there will be no dazzling of eyes that must be able to detect the minutest specks of white light on a navigating vision plate. There were aliens waiting to receive them. They blinked at the brightness of the helmet lights. The space-phone receivers said in Tommy's ear:

'They say, sir, their skipper is waiting for you.'

Tommy and the skipper were in a long corridor with a soft flooring underfoot. Their lights showed details of which every one was exotic.

'I think I'll crack my helmet, sir,' said Tommy.

He did. The air was good. By analysis it was thirty per cent oxygen instead of twenty for normal air on Earth, but the pressure was less. It felt just right. The artificial gravity, too, was less than that maintained on the *Llanvabon*. The home planet of the aliens would be smaller than Earth, and – by the infrared data – circling close to a nearly dead, dull-red sun. The air had smells in it. They were utterly strange, but not unpleasant.

An arched opening. A ramp with the same soft stuff underfoot. Lights which actually shed a dim, dull-red glow about. The aliens had stepped up some of their illuminating equipment as an act of courtesy. The light might hurt their eyes, but it was a gesture of consideration which made Tommy even more anxious for his plan to go through.

The alien skipper faced them with what seemed to Tommy a gesture of wryly humorous deprecation. The helmet phones said:

'He says, sir, that he greets you with pleasure, but he has been able to think of only one way in which the problem created by the meeting of these two ships can be solved.'

'He means a fight,' said the skipper. 'Tell him I'm here to offer another choice.'

The *Llanvabon*'s skipper and the skipper of the alien ship were face to face, but their communication was weirdly indirect. The aliens used no sound in communication. Their talk, in fact, took place on microwaves and approximated telepathy. But they could not hear, in any ordinary sense of the word, so the skipper's and Tommy's speech approached telepathy, too, as far as they were concerned. When the skipper spoke, his space phone sent his words back to the *Llanvabon*, where the words were fed into the coder and short-wave equivalents sent back to the black ship. The alien skipper's reply went to the *Llanvabon* and through the decoder, and was retransmitted by space phone in words read from the message frame. It was awkward, but it worked.

*

The short and stocky alien skipper paused. The helmet phones relayed his translated, soundless reply.

'He is anxious to hear, sir.'

The skipper took off his helmet. He put his hands at his belt in a belligerent pose.

'Look here!' he said truculently to the bald, strange creature in the unearthly red glow before him. 'It looks like we have to fight and one batch of us get killed. We're ready to do it if we have to. But if you win, we've got it fixed so you'll never find out where Earth is, and there's a good chance we'll get you anyhow! If we win, we'll be in the same fix. And if we win and go back home, our government will fit out a fleet and start hunting your planet. And if we find it we'll be ready to blast it to hell! If you win, the same thing will happen to us! And it's all foolishness! We've stayed here a month, and we've swapped information, and we don't hate each other. There's no reason for us to fight except for the rest of our respective races!'

The skipper stopped for breath, scowling. Tommy Dort inconspicuously put his own hands on the belt of his spacesuit. He waited, hoping desperately that the trick would work.

'He says, sir,' reported the helmet phones, 'that all you say is true. But that his race has to be protected, just as you feel that yours must be.'

'Naturally!' said the skipper angrily, 'but the sensible thing to do is to figure out how to protect it! Putting its future up as a gamble in a fight is not sensible. Our races have to be warned of each other's existence. That's true. But each should have proof that the other doesn't want to fight, but wants to be friendly. And we shouldn't be able to find each other, but we should be able to communicate with each other to work out grounds for a common trust. If our governments want to be fools, let them! But we should give them the chance to make friends, instead of starting a space war out of mutual funk!'

Briefly, the space phone said:

'He says that the difficulty is that of trusting each other

now. With the possible existence of his race at stake, he cannot take any chance, and neither can you, of yielding an advantage.'

'But my race,' boomed the skipper, glaring at the alien captain, 'my race has an advantage now. We came here to your ship in atom-powered spacesuits! Before we left, we altered the drives! We can set off ten pounds of sensitized fuel apiece, right here in this ship, or it can be set off by remote control from our ship! It will be rather remarkable if your fuel store doesn't blow up with us! In other words, if you don't accept my proposal for a commonsense approach to this predicament, Dort and I blow up in an atomic explosion, and your ship will be wrecked if not destroyed – and the *Llanvabon* will be attacking with everything it's got within two seconds after the blast goes off!'

The captain's room of the alien ship was a strange scene, with its dull-red illumination and the strange, bald, gill-breathing aliens watching the skipper and waiting for the inaudible translation of the harangue they could not hear. But a sudden tensity appeared in the air. A sharp, savage feeling of strain. The alien skipper made a gesture. The helmet phones hummed.

'He says, sir, what is your proposal?'

'Swap ships!' roared the skipper. 'Swap ships and go on home! We can fix our instruments so they'll do no trailing, he can do the same with his. We'll each remove our star maps and records. We'll each dismantle our weapons. The air will serve, and we'll take their ship and they'll take ours, and neither one can harm or trail the other, and each will carry home more information than can be taken otherwise! We can agree on this same Crab Nebula as a rendezvous when the double-star has made another circuit, and if our people want to meet them they can do it, and if they are scared they can duck it! That's my proposal! And he'll take it, or Dort and I blow up their ship and the *Llanvabon* blasts what's left!'

He glared about him while he waited for the translation to reach the tense small stocky figures about him. He could tell when it came because the tenseness changed. The figures stirred. They made gestures. One of them made convulsive movements. It lay down on the soft floor and kicked. Others leaned against its walls and shook.

The voice in Tommy Dort's helmet phones had been strictly crisp and professional, before, but now it sounded blankly amazed.

'He says, sir, that it is a good joke. Because the two crew members he sent to our ship, and that you passed on the way, have their spacesuits stuffed with atomic explosive too, sir, and he intended to make the very same offer and threat! Of course he accepts, sir. Your ship is worth more to him than his own, and his is worth more to you than the *Llanvabon*. It appears, sir, to be a deal.'

Then Tommy Dort realized what the convulsive movements of the aliens were. They were laughter.

It wasn't quite as simple as the skipper had outlined it. The actual working-out of the proposal was complicated. For three days the crews of the two ships were intermingled, the aliens learning the workings of the *Llanvabon*'s engines, and the men learning the controls of the black spaceship. It was a good joke – but it wasn't all a joke. There were men on the black ship, and aliens on the *Llanvabon*, ready at an instant's notice to blow up the vessels in question. And they would have done it in case of need, for which reason the need did not appear. But it was, actually, a better arrangement to have two expeditions return to two civilizations, under the current arrangement, than for either to return alone.

There were differences, though. There was some dispute about the removal of records. In most cases the dispute was settled by the destruction of the records. There was more trouble caused by the *Llanvabon*'s books, and the alien equivalent of a ship's library, containing works which approximated the novels of Earth. But those items were valuable to possible friendship, because they would show the two cultures, each to the other, from the viewpoint of normal citizens and without propaganda.

But nerves were tense during those three days. Aliens unloaded and inspected the foodstuffs intended for the men on the black ship. Men transshipped the foodstuffs the aliens would need to return to their home. There were endless details, from exchange of lighting equipment to suit the eyesight of the exchanging crews, to a final check-up of apparatus. A joint inspection party of both races verified that all detector devices had been smashed but not removed, so that they could not be used for trailing and had not been smuggled away. And of course, the aliens were anxious not to leave any useful weapon on the black ship, nor the men upon the *Llanvabon*. It was a curious fact that each crew was best qualified to take exactly the measures which made an evasion of the agreement impossible.

There was a final conference before the two ships parted, back in the communications room of the *Llanvabon*.

'Tell the little runt,' rumbled the *Llanvabon*'s former skipper, 'that he's got a good ship and he'd better treat her right.'

The message frame flicked word-cards into position.

'I believe,' it said on the alien skipper's behalf, 'that your ship is just as good. I will hope to meet you here when the double star has turned one turn.'

The last man left the *Llanvabon*. It moved away into the misty nebula before they had returned to the black ship. The vision plates in that vessel had been altered for human eyes, and human crewmen watched jealously for any trace of their former ship as their new craft took a crazy, evading course to a remote part of the nebula. It came to a crevasse of nothingness, leading to the stars. It rose swiftly to clear space. There was the instant of breathlessness which the overdrive field produces as it goes on, and then the black ship whipped away into the void at many times the speed of light.

Many days later, the skipper saw Tommy Dort poring over one of the strange objects which were the equivalent of books. It was fascinating to puzzle over. The skipper was pleased with himself. The technicians of the *Llanvabon*'s former crew were finding out desirable things about the ship almost momently. Doubtless the aliens were as pleased with their discoveries in the *Llanvabon*. But the black ship would be enormously worth while – and the solution that had been found was by any standard much superior even to a combat in which the Earthmen had been overwhelmingly victorious.

'Hm-m-m. Mr Dort,' said the skipper profoundly. 'You've no equipment to make another photographic record on the way back. It was left on the *Llanvabon*. But fortunately, we have your record taken on the way out, and I shall report most favourably on your suggestion and your assistance in carrying it out. I think very well of you, sir.'

'Thank you, sir,' said Tommy Dort.

He waited. The skipper cleared his throat.

'You . . . ah . . . first realized the close similarity of mental processes between the aliens and ourselves,' he observed. 'What do you think of the prospects of a friendly arrangement if we keep a rendezvous with them at the nebula as agreed?'

'Oh, we'll get along all right, sir,' said Tommy. 'We've got a good start towards friendship. After all, since they see by infrared, the planets they'd want to make use of wouldn't suit us. There's no reason why we shouldn't get along. We're almost alike in psychology.'

'Hm-m-m. Now just what do you mean by that?' demanded the skipper.

'Why, they're just like us, sir!' said Tommy. 'Of course they breathe through gills and they see by heat waves, and their blood has a copper base instead of iron and a few little details like that. But otherwise we're just alike! There were only men in their crew, sir, but they have two sexes as we have, and they have families, and . . . er . . . their sense of humour – In fact – '

Tommy hesitated.

'Go on, sir,' said the skipper.

'Well – There was the one I called Buck, sir, because he hasn't any name that goes into sound waves,' said Tommy.

'We got along very well. I'd really call him my friend, sir. And we were together for a couple of hours just before the two ships separated and we'd nothing in particular to do. So I became convinced that humans and aliens are bound to be good friends if they have only half a chance. You see, sir, we spent those two hours telling dirty jokes.'

THE BIG FRONT YARD

by Clifford Simak

Hiram Taine came awake and sat up in his bed.

Towser was barking and scratching at the floor.

'Shut up,' Taine told the dog.

Towser cocked quizzical ears at him and then resumed the barking and scratching at the floor.

Taine rubbed his eyes. He ran a hand through his rat's-nest head of hair. He considered lying down again and pulling up the covers.

But not with Towser barking.

'What's the matter with you, anyhow?' he asked Towser, with not a little wrath.

'*Whuff*,' said Towser, industriously proceeding with his scratching at the floor.

'If you want out,' said Taine, 'all you got to do is open the screen door. You know how it is done. You do it all the time.'

Towser quit his barking and sat down heavily, watching his master getting out of bed.

Taine put on his shirt and pulled on his trousers, but didn't bother with his shoes.

Towser ambled over to a corner, put his nose down to the baseboard and snuffled moistly.

'You got a mouse?' asked Taine.

'*Whuff*,' said Towser, most emphatically.

'I can't ever remember you making such a row about a mouse,' Taine said, slightly puzzled. 'You must be off your rocker.'

It was a beautiful summer morning. Sunlight was pouring through the open window.

Good day for fishing, Taine told himself, then remembered

that there'd be no fishing, for he had to go out and look up that old four-poster maple bed that he had heard about up Woodman way. More than likely, he thought, they'd want twice as much as it was worth. It was getting so, he told himself, that a man couldn't make an honest dollar. Everyone was getting smart about antiques.

He got up off the bed and headed for the living-room.

'Come on,' he said to Towser.

Towser came along, pausing now and then to snuffle into corners and to whuffle at the floor.

'You got it bad,' said Taine.

Maybe it's a rat, he thought. The house was getting old.

He opened the screen door and Towser went outside.

'Leave that woodchuck be today,' Taine advised him. 'It's a losing battle. You'll never dig him out.'

Towser went around the corner of the house.

Taine noticed that something had happened to the sign that hung on the post beside the driveway. One of the chains had become unhooked and the sign was dangling.

He padded out across the driveway slab and the grass, still wet with dew, to fix the sign. There was nothing wrong with it – just the unhooked chain. Might have been the wind, he thought, or some passing urchin. Although probably not an urchin. He got along with kids. They never bothered him, like they did some others in the village. Banker Stevens, for example. They were always pestering Stevens.

He stood back a way to be sure the sign was straight.

It read, in big letters:

HANDY-MAN

And under that, in smaller lettering:

I fix anything

And under that:

ANTIQUES FOR SALE
What have you got to trade?

Maybe, he told himself, he ought to have two signs, one for his fix-it shop and one for antiques and trading. Some day, when he had the time, he thought, he'd paint a couple of new ones, one for each side of the driveway. It would look neat that way.

He turned around and looked across the road at Turner's Woods. It was a pretty sight, he thought. A sizeable piece of woods like that right at the edge of town. It was a place for birds and rabbits and woodchucks and squirrels and it was full of forts built through generations by the boys of Willow Bend.

Some day, of course, some smart operator would buy it up and start a housing development or something equally objectionable and when that happened a big slice of his own boyhood would be cut out of his life.

Towser came around the corner of the house. He was sidling along, sniffing at the lowest row of siding and his ears were cocked with interest.

'That dog is nuts,' said Taine and went inside.

He went into the kitchen, his bare feet slapping on the floor.

He filled the tea-kettle, set it on the stove and turned the burner on underneath the kettle.

He turned on the radio, forgetting that it was out of kilter.

When it didn't make a sound, he remembered and, disgusted, snapped it off. That was the way it went, he thought. He fixed other people's stuff, but never got around to fixing any of his own.

He went into the bedroom and put on his shoes. He threw the bed together.

Back in the kitchen the stove had failed to work again. The burner beneath the kettle was still cold.

Taine hauled off and kicked the stove. He lifted the kettle and held his palm above the burner. In a few seconds he could detect some heat.

'Worked again,' he told himself.

Some day, he knew, kicking the stove would fail to work. When that happened, he'd have to get to work on it. Probably wasn't more than a loose connection.

He put the kettle back on to the stove.

There was a clatter out in front and Taine went out to see what was going on.

Beasly, the Hortons' yardboy-chauffeur-gardener-et cetera, was backing a rickety old truck up the driveway. Beside him sat Abbie Horton, the wife of H. Henry Horton, the village's most important citizen. In the back of the truck, lashed on with ropes and half-protected by a garish red and purple quilt, stood a mammoth television set. Taine recognized it from of old. It was a good ten years out of date and still, by any standard, it was the most expensive set ever to grace any home in Willow Bend.

Abbie hopped out of the truck. She was an energetic, bustling, bossy woman.

'Good morning, Hiram,' she said. 'Can you fix this set again?'

'Never saw anything that I couldn't fix,' said Taine, but nevertheless he eyed the set with something like dismay. It was not the first time he had tangled with it and he knew what was ahead.

'It might cost you more than it's worth,' he warned her. 'What you really need is a new one. This set is getting old and – '

'That's just what Henry said,' Abbie told him, tartly. 'Henry wants to get one of the colour sets. But I won't part with this one. It's not just TV, you know. It's a combination with radio and a record player and the wood and style are just right for the other furniture, and besides – '

'Yes, I know,' said Taine, who'd heard it all before.

Poor old Henry, he thought. What a life the man must lead. Up at that computer plant all day long, shooting off his face and bossing everyone, then coming home to a life of petty tyranny.

'Beasly,' said Abbie, in her best drill-sergeant voice, 'you get right up there and get that thing untied.'

'Yes'm,' Beasly said. He was a gangling, loose-jointed man

who didn't look too bright.

'And see you be careful with it. I don't want it all scratched up.'

'Yes'm,' said Beasly.

'I'll help,' Taine offered.

The two climbed into the truck and began unlashing the old monstrosity.

'It's heavy,' Abbie warned. 'You two be careful of it.'

'Yes'm,' said Beasly.

It was heavy and it was an awkward thing to boot, but Beasly and Taine horsed it around to the back of the house and up the stoop and through the back door and down the basement stairs, with Abbie following eagle-eyed behind them, alert to the slightest scratch.

The basement was Taine's combination workshop and display-room for antiques. One end of it was filled with benches and with tools and machinery, and boxes full of odds and ends and piles of just plain junk were scattered everywhere. The other end housed a collection of rickety chairs, sagging bed-posts, ancient highboys, equally ancient lowboys, old coal scuttles painted gold, heavy iron fireplace screens, and a lot of other stuff that he had collected from far and wide for as little as he could possibly pay for it.

He and Beasly set the TV down carefully on the floor. Abbie watched them narrowly from the stairs.

'Why, Hiram,' she said, excited, 'you put a ceiling in the basement. It looks a whole lot better.'

'Huh?' asked Taine.

'The ceiling. I said you put in a ceiling.'

Taine jerked his head up and what she said was true. There was a ceiling there, but he'd never put it in.

He gulped a little and lowered his head, then jerked it quickly up and had another look. The ceiling was still there.

'It's not that block stuff,' said Abbie with open admiration. 'You can't see any joints at all. How did you manage it?'

Taine gulped again and got back his voice. 'Something I

thought up,' he told her weakly.

'You'll have to come over and do it to our basement. Our basement is a sight. Beasly put the ceiling in the amusement-room, but Beasly is all thumbs.'

'Yes'm,' Beasly said contritely.

'When I get the time,' Taine promised, ready to promise anything to get them out of there.

'You'd have a lot more time,' Abbie told him acidly, 'if you weren't gadding around all over the country buying up that broken-down old furniture that you call antiques. Maybe you can fool the city folks when they come driving out here, but you can't fool me.'

'I can make a lot of money out of some of it,' Taine told her calmly.

'And lose your shirt on the rest of it,' she said.

'I got some old china that is just the kind of stuff you are looking for,' said Taine. 'Picked it up just a day or two ago. Made a good buy on it. I can let you have it cheap.'

'I'm not interested,' she said and clamped her mouth tight shut.

She turned around and went back up the stairs.

'She's on the prod today,' Beasly said to Taine. 'It will be a bad day. It always is when she starts early in the morning.'

'Don't pay attention to her,' Taine advised.

'I try not to, but it ain't possible. You sure you don't need a man? I'd work for you cheap.'

'Sorry, Beasly. Tell you what – come over some night soon and we'll play some chequers.'

'I'll do that, Hiram. You're the only one who ever asks me over. All the others ever do is laugh at me or shout.'

Abbie's voice came bellowing down the stairs. 'Beasly, are you coming? Don't go standing there all day. I have rugs to beat.'

'Yes'm,' said Beasly, starting up the stairs.

At the truck, Abbie turned on Taine with determination: 'You'll get that set fixed right away? I'm lost without it.'

'Immediately,' said Taine.

He stood and watched them off, then looked around for Towser, but the dog had disappeared. More than likely he was at the woodchuck hole again, in the woods across the road. Gone off, thought Taine, without his breakfast, too.

The tea-kettle was boiling furiously when Taine got back to the kitchen. He put coffee in the maker and poured in the water. Then he went downstairs.

The ceiling was still there.

He turned on all the lights and walked around the basement staring up at it.

It was a dazzling white material and it appeared to be translucent – up to a point, that is, one could see into it, but one could not see through it. And there were no signs of seams. It was fitted neatly and tightly around the water pipes and the ceiling lights.

Taine stood on a chair and rapped his knuckles against it sharply. It gave out a bell-like sound, almost exactly as if he'd rapped a fingernail against a thinly-blown goblet.

He got down off the chair and stood there, shaking his head. The whole thing was beyond him. He had spent part of the evening repairing Banker Stevens's lawn-mower and there'd been no ceiling then.

He rummaged in a box and found a drill. He dug out one of the smaller bits and fitted it in the drill. He plugged in the cord and climbed on the chair again and tried the bit against the ceiling. The whirling steel slid wildly back and forth. It didn't make a scratch. He switched off the drill and looked closely at the ceiling. There was not a mark upon it. He tried again, pressing against the drill with all his strength. The bit went *ping* and the broken end flew across the basement and hit the wall.

Taine stepped down off the chair. He found another bit and fitted it in the drill and went slowly up the stairs, trying to think. But he was too confused to think. That ceiling should not be up there, but there it was. And unless he went stark, staring crazy and forgetful as well, he had not put it there.

In the living-room, he folded back one corner of the worn

and faded carpeting and plugged in the drill. He knelt and started drilling in the floor. The bit went smoothly through the old oak flooring, then stopped. He put on more pressure and the drill spun without getting any bite.

And there wasn't supposed to be anything underneath that wood! Nothing to stop a drill. Once through the flooring, it should have dropped into the space between the joists.

Taine disengaged the drill and laid it to one side.

He went into the kitchen and the coffee now was ready. But before he poured it, he pawed through a cabinet drawer and found a pencil flashlight. Back in the living-room he shone the light into the hole that the drill had made.

There was something shiny at the bottom of the hole.

He went back to the kitchen and found some day-old doughnuts and poured a cup of coffee. He sat at the kitchen table, eating doughnuts and wondering what to do.

There didn't appear, for the moment at least, much that he could do. He could putter around all day trying to figure out what had happened to his basement and probably not be any wiser than he was right now.

His money-making Yankee soul rebelled against such a horrid waste of time.

There was, he told himself, that maple four-poster that he should be getting to before some unprincipled city antique dealer should run afoul of it. A piece like that, he figured, if a man had any luck at all, should sell at a right good price. He might turn a handsome profit on it if he only worked it right.

Maybe, he thought, he could turn a trade on it. There was the table model TV set that he traded a pair of ice skates for last winter. Those folks out Woodman way might conceivably be happy to trade the bed for a reconditioned TV set, almost like brand new. After all, they probably weren't using the bed and, he hoped fervently, had no idea of the value of it.

He ate the doughnuts hurriedly and gulped down an extra cup of coffee. He fixed a plate of scraps for Towser and set it outside the door. Then he went down into the basement and got the table TV set and put it in the pick-up truck. As an afterthought, he added a reconditioned shotgun which would be perfectly all right if a man were careful not to use these far-reaching, powerful shells, and a few other odds and ends that might come in handy on a trade.

He got back late, for it had been a busy and quite satisfactory day. Not only did he have the four-poster loaded on the truck, but he had as well a rocking chair, a fire-screen, a bundle of ancient magazines, an old-fashioned barrel churn, a walnut highboy and a Governor Winthrop on which some half-baked, slap-happy decorator had applied a coat of apple-green paint. The television set, the shotgun and five dollars had gone into the trade. And what was better yet, he'd managed it so well that the Woodman family probably was dying of laughter at this very moment about how they'd taken him.

He felt a little ashamed of it – they'd been such friendly people. They had treated him so kindly and had him stay for dinner and had sat and talked with him and shown him about the farm and even asked him to stop by if he went through that way again.

He'd wasted the entire day, he thought, and he rather hated that, but maybe it had been worth it to build up his reputation out that way as the sort of character who had softening of the head and didn't know the value of a dollar. That way, maybe some other day, he could do some more business in the neighbourhood.

He heard the television set as he opened the back door, sounding loud and clear, and he went clattering down the basement stairs in something close to a panic. For now that he'd traded off the table model, Abbie's set was the only one downstairs and Abbie's set was broken.

It was Abbie's set, all right. It stood just where he and Beasly had put it down that morning and there was nothing wrong with it – nothing wrong at all. It was even televising colour.

Televising colour!

He stopped at the bottom of the stairs and leaned against

the railing for support.

The set kept right on televising colour.

Taine stalked the set and walked around behind it.

The back of the cabinet was off, leaning against a bench that stood behind the set, and he could see the innards of it glowing cheerily.

He squatted on the basement floor and squinted at the lighted innards and they seemed a good deal different from the way that they should be. He'd repaired the set many times before and he thought he had a good idea of what the working parts would look like. And now they all seemed different, although just how he couldn't tell.

A heavy step sounded on the stairs and a hearty voice came booming down to him.

'Well, Hiram, I see you got it fixed.'

Taine jack-knifed upright and stood there slightly frozen and completely speechless.

Henry Horton stood four-squarely and happily on the stairs, looking very pleased.

'I told Abbie that you wouldn't have it done, but she said for me to come over anyway – Hey, Hiram, it's in colour! How did you do it, man?'

Taine grinned sickly. 'I just got fiddling around,' he said.

Henry came down the rest of the stairs with a stately step and stood before the set, with his hands behind his back, staring at it fixedly in his best executive manner.

He slowly shook his head. 'I never would have thought,' he said, 'that it was possible.'

'Abbie mentioned that you wanted colour.'

'Well, sure. Of course I did. But not on this old set. I never would have expected to get colour on this set. How did you do it, Hiram?'

Taine told the solemn truth. 'I can't rightly say,' he said.

Henry found a nail keg standing in front of one of the benches and rolled it out in front of the old-fashioned set. He sat down warily and relaxed into solid comfort.

'That's the way it goes,' he said. 'There are men like you,

but not very many of them. Just Yankee tinkerers. You keep messing around with things, trying one thing here and another there and before you know it you come up with something.'

He sat on the nail keg, staring at the set.

'It's sure a pretty thing,' he said. 'It's better than the colour they have in Minneapolis. I dropped in at a couple of the places the last time I was there and looked at the colour sets. And I tell you honest, Hiram, there wasn't one of them that was as good as this.'

Taine wiped his brow with his shirt sleeve. Somehow or other, the basement seemed to be getting warm. He was fine sweat all over.

Henry found a big cigar in one of his pockets and held it out to Taine.

'No, thanks. I never smoke.'

'Perhaps you're wise,' said Henry. 'It's a nasty habit.'

He stuck the cigar into his mouth and rolled it east to west.

'Each man to his own,' he proclaimed expansively. 'When it comes to a thing like this, you're the man to do it. You seem to think in mechanical contraptions and electronic circuits. Me, I don't know a thing about it. Even in the computer game, I still don't know a thing about it; I hire men who do. I can't even saw a board or drive a nail. But I can organize. You remember, Hiram, how everybody snickered when I started up the plant?'

'Well, I guess some of them did, at that.'

'You're darn tooting they did. They went around for weeks with their hands up to their faces to hide smart-aleck grins. They said, what does Henry think he's doing, starting up a computer factory out here in the sticks; he doesn't think he can compete with those big companies in the east, does he? And they didn't stop their grinning until I sold a couple of dozen units and had orders for a year or two ahead.'

He fished a lighter from his pocket and lit the cigar carefully, never taking his eyes off the television set.

'You got something there,' he said, judiciously, 'that may be worth a mint of money. Some simple adaptation that will fit on any set. If you can get colour on this old wreck, you can get colour on any set that's made.'

He chuckled moistly around the mouthful of cigar. 'If RCA knew what was happening here this minute, they'd go out and cut their throats.'

'But I don't know what I did,' protested Taine.

'Well, that's all right,' said Henry, happily. 'I'll take this set up to the plant tomorrow and turn loose some of the boys on it. They'll find out what you have here before they're through with it.'

He took the cigar out of his mouth and studied it intently, then popped it back in again.

'As I was saying, Hiram, that's the difference in us. You can do the stuff, but you miss the possibilities. I can't do a thing, but I can organize it once the thing is done. Before we get through with this, you'll be wading in twenty-dollar bills clear up to your knees.'

'But I don't have – '

'Don't worry. Just leave it all to me. I've got the plant and whatever money we may need. We'll figure out a split.'

'That's fine of you,' said Taine mechanically.

'Not at all,' Henry insisted, grandly. 'It's just my aggressive, grasping sense of profit. I should be ashamed of myself, cutting in on this.'

He sat on the keg, smoking and watching the TV perform in exquisite colour.

'You know, Hiram,' he said, 'I've often thought of this, but never got around to doing anything about it. I've got an old computer up at the plant that we will have to junk because it's taking up room that we really need. It's one of our early models, a sort of experimental job that went completely sour. It sure is a screwy thing. No one's ever been able to make much out of it. We tried some approaches that probably were wrong – or maybe they were right, but we didn't know enough to make them quite come off. It's been standing in a corner all these years and I should have junked it long ago. But I sort of hate to do it. I wonder if you might not like it – just to tinker with.'

'Well, I don't know,' said Taine.

Henry assumed an expansive air. 'No obligation, mind you. You may not be able to do a thing with it – I'd frankly be surprised if you could, but there's no harm in trying. Maybe you'll decide to tear it down for the salvage you can get. There are several thousand dollars' worth of equipment in it. Probably you could use most of it one way or another.'

'It might be interesting,' conceded Taine, but not too enthusiastically.

'Good,' said Henry, with an enthusiasm that made up for Taine's lack of it. 'I'll have the boys cart it over tomorrow. It's a heavy thing. I'll send along plenty of help to get it unloaded and down into the basement and set up.'

Henry stood up carefully and brushed cigar ashes off his lap.

'I'll have the boys pick up the TV set at the same time,' he said. 'I'll have to tell Abbie you haven't got it fixed yet. If I ever let it get into the house, the way it's working now, she'd hold on to it.'

Henry climbed the stairs heavily and Taine saw him out of the door into the summer night.

Taine stood in the shadow, watching Henry's shadowed figure go across the Widow Taylor's yard to the next street behind his house. He took a deep breath of the fresh night air and shook his head to try to clear his buzzing brain, but the buzzing went right on.

Too much had happened, he told himself. Too much for any single day – first the ceiling and now the TV set. Once he had a good night's sleep he might be in some sort of shape to try to wrestle with it.

Towser came around the corner of the house and limped slowly up the steps to stand beside his master. He was mud up to his ears.

'You had a day of it, I see,' said Taine. 'And, just like I told you, you didn't get the woodchuck.'

'*Woof*,' said Towser, sadly.

'You're just like a lot of the rest of us,' Taine told him, severely. 'Like me and Henry Horton and all the rest of us. You're chasing something and you think you know what you're chasing, but you really don't. And what's even worse, you have no faint idea of why you're chasing it.'

Towser thumped a tired tail upon the stoop.

Taine opened the door and stood to one side to let Towser in, then went in himself.

He went through the refrigerator and found part of a roast, a slice or two of luncheon-meat, a dried-out slab of cheese and half a bowl of cooked spaghetti. He made a pot of coffee and shared the food with Towser.

Then Taine went back downstairs and shut off the television set. He found a trouble lamp and plugged it in and poked the light into the innards of the set.

He squatted on the floor, holding the lamp, trying to puzzle out what had been done to the set. It was different, of course, but it was a little hard to figure out in just what ways it was different. Someone had tinkered with the tubes and had them twisted out of shape and there were little white cubes of metal tucked here and there in what seemed to be an entirely haphazard and illogical manner – although, Taine admitted to himself, there probably was no haphazardness. And the circuit, he saw, had been rewired and a good deal of wiring had been added.

But the most puzzling thing about it was that the whole thing seemed to be just jury-rigged – as if someone had done no more than a hurried, patch-up job to get the set back in working order on an emergency and temporary basis.

Someone, he thought!

And who had that someone been?

He hunched around and peered into the dark corners of the basement and he felt innumerable and many-legged imaginary insects running on his body.

Someone had taken the back off the cabinet and leaned it against the bench and had left the screws which held the back laid neatly in a row upon the floor. Then they had jury-rigged the set and jury-rigged it far better than it had ever been before.

If this was a jury-job, he wondered, just what kind of job would it have been if they had had the time to do it up in style?

They hadn't had the time, of course. Maybe they had been scared off when he had come home – scared off even before they could get the back on the set again.

He stood up and moved stiffly away.

First the ceiling in the morning – and now, in the evening, Abbie's television set.

And the ceiling, come to think of it, was not a ceiling only. Another liner, if that was the proper term for it, of the same material as the ceiling had been laid beneath the floor, forming a sort of boxed-in area between the joists. He had struck that liner when he had tried to drill into the floor.

And what, he asked himself, if all the house were like that, too?

There was just one answer to it all: *There was something in the house with him!*

Towser had heard that *something* or smelled it or in some other manner sensed it and had dug frantically at the floor in an attempt to dig it out, as if it were a woodchuck.

Except that this, whatever it might be, certainly was no woodchuck.

He put away the trouble light and went upstairs.

Towser was curled up on a rug in the living-room beside the easy-chair and beat his tail in polite decorum in greeting to his master.

Taine stood and stared down at the dog. Towser looked back at him with satisfied and sleepy eyes, then heaved a doggish sigh and settled down to sleep.

Whatever Towser might have heard or smelled or sensed this morning, it was quite evident that as of this moment he was aware of it no longer.

Then Taine remembered something else.

He had filled the kettle to make water for the coffee and had set it on the stove. He had turned on the burner and it had worked the first time.

He hadn't had to kick the stove to get the burner going.

He woke in the morning and someone was holding down his feet and he sat up quickly to see what was going on.

But there was nothing to be alarmed about; it was only Towser who had crawled into bed with him and now lay sprawled across his feet.

Towser whined softly and his back legs twitched as he chased dream rabbits.

Taine eased his feet from beneath the dog and sat up, reaching for his clothes. It was early, but he remembered suddenly that he had left all of the furniture he had picked up the day before out there in the truck and should be getting downstairs where he could start reconditioning it.

Towser went on sleeping.

Taine stumbled to the kitchen and looked out of the window and there, squatted on the back stoop, was Beasly, the Horton man-of-all-work.

Taine went to the back door to see what was going on.

'I quit them, Hiram,' Beasly told him. 'She kept on pecking at me every minute of the day and I couldn't do a thing to please her, so I up and quit.'

'Well, come on in,' said Taine. 'I suppose you'd like a bite to eat and a cup of coffee.'

'I was kind of wondering if I could stay here, Hiram. Just for my keep until I can find something else.'

'Let's have breakfast first,' said Taine, 'then we can talk about it.'

He didn't like it, he told himself. He didn't like it at all. In another hour or so Abbie would show up and start stirring up a ruckus about how he'd lured Beasly off. Because, no matter how dumb Beasly might be, he did a lot of work and took a lot of nagging and there wasn't anyone else in town who would work for Abbie Horton.

'Your ma used to give me cookies all the time,' said Beasly. 'Your ma was a real good woman, Hiram.'

'Yes, she was,' said Taine.

'My ma used to say that you folks were quality, not like the rest in town, no matter what kind of airs they were always putting on. She said your family was among the first settlers. Is that really true, Hiram?'

'Well, not exactly first settlers, I guess, but this house has stood here for almost a hundred years. My father used to say there never was a night during all those years that there wasn't at least one Taine beneath its roof. Things like that, it seems, meant a lot to Father.'

'It must be nice,' said Beasly, wistfully, 'to have a feeling like that. You must be proud of this house, Hiram.'

'Not really proud; more like belonging. I can't imagine living in any other house.'

Taine turned on the burner and filled the kettle. Carrying the kettle back, he kicked the stove. But there wasn't any need to kick it; the burner was already beginning to take on a rosy glow.

Twice in a row, Taine thought. This thing is getting better!

'Gee, Hiram,' said Beasly, 'this is a dandy radio.'

'It's no good,' said Taine. 'It's broke. Haven't had the time to fix it.'

'I don't think so, Hiram. I just turned it on. It's beginning to warm up.'

'It's beginning to – Hey, let me see!' yelled Taine.

Beasly told the truth. A faint hum was coming from the tubes.

A voice came in, gaining in volume as the set warmed up.

It was speaking gibberish.

'What kind of talk is that?' asked Beasly.

'I don't know,' said Taine, close to panic now.

First the television set, then the stove and now the radio!

He spun the tuning knob and the pointer crawled slowly across the dial face instead of spinning across as he remembered it, and station after station sputtered and went past.

He tuned in the next station that came up and it was strange lingo, too – and he knew by then exactly what he had.

Instead of a $39.50 job, he had here on the kitchen table an all-band receiver like they advertised in the fancy magazines.

He straightened up and said to Beasly: 'See if you can get someone speaking English. I'll get on with the eggs.'

He turned on the second burner and got out the frying-pan. He put it on the stove and found eggs and bacon in the refrigerator.

Beasly got a station that had band music playing.

'How's that?' he asked.

'That's fine,' said Taine.

Towser came out from the bedroom, stretching and yawning. He went to the door and showed he wanted out.

Taine let him out.

'If I were you,' he told the dog, 'I'd lay off that woodchuck. You'll have all the woods dug up.'

'He ain't digging after any woodchuck, Hiram.'

'Well, a rabbit, then.'

'Not a rabbit, either. I snuck off yesterday when I was supposed to be beating rugs. That's what Abbie got so sore about.'

Taine grunted, breaking eggs into the skillet.

'I snuck away and went over to where Towser was. I talked with him and he told me it wasn't a woodchuck or a rabbit. He said it was something else. I pitched in and helped him dig. Looks to me like he found an old tank of some sort buried out there in the woods.'

'Towser wouldn't dig up any tank,' protested Taine. 'He wouldn't care about anything except a rabbit or a woodchuck.'

'He was working hard,' insisted Beasly. 'He seemed to be excited.'

'Maybe the woodchuck just dug his hole under this old tank or whatever it might be.'

'Maybe so,' Beasly agreed. He fiddled with the radio some more. He got a disc jockey who was pretty terrible.

Taine shovelled eggs and bacon on to plates and brought them to the table. He poured big cups of coffee and began buttering the toast.

'Dive in,' he said to Beasly.

'This is good of you, Hiram, to take me in like this. I won't stay no longer than it takes to find a job.'

'Well, I didn't exactly say – '

'There are times,' said Beasly, 'when I get to thinking I haven't got a friend and then I remember your ma, how nice she was to me and all – '

'Oh, all right,' said Taine.

He knew when he was licked.

He brought the toast and a jar of jam to the table and sat down, beginning to eat.

'Maybe you got something I could help you with,' suggested Beasly, using the back of his hand to wipe egg off his chin.

'I have a load of furniture out in the driveway. I could use a man to help me get it down into the basement.'

'I'll be glad to do that,' said Beasly. 'I am good and strong. I don't mind work at all. I just don't like people jawing at me.'

They finished breakfast and then carried the furniture down into the basement. They had some trouble with the Governor Winthrop, for it was an unwieldy thing to handle.

When they finally horsed it down, Taine stood off and looked at it. The man, he told himself, who slapped paint on to that beautiful cherrywood had a lot to answer for.

He said to Beasly: 'We have to get the paint off that thing there. And we must do it carefully. Use paint remover and a rag wrapped around a spatula and just sort of roll it off. Would you like to try it?'

'Sure, I would. Say, Hiram, what will we have for lunch?'

'I don't know,' said Taine. 'We'll throw something together. Don't tell me you're hungry.'

'Well, it was sort of hard work, getting all that stuff down here.'

'There are cookies in the jar on the kitchen shelf,' said Taine. 'Go and help yourself.'

When Beasly went upstairs, Taine walked slowly around the basement. The ceiling, he saw, was still intact. Nothing else seemed to be disturbed.

Maybe that television set and the stove and radio, he

thought, was just their way of paying rent to me. And if that were the case, he told himself, whoever they might be, he'd be more than willing to let them stay right on.

He looked around some more and could find nothing wrong.

He went upstairs and called to Beasly in the kitchen.

'Come on out to the garage, where I keep the paint. We'll hunt up some remover and show you how to use it.'

Beasly, a supply of cookies clutched in his hand, trotted willingly behind him.

As they rounded the corner of the house they could hear Towser's muffled barking. Listening to him, it seemed to Taine that he was getting hoarse.

Three days, he thought – or was it four?

'If we don't do something about it,' he said, 'that fool dog is going to get himself wore out.'

He went into the garage and came back with two shovels and a pick.

'Come on,' he said to Beasly. 'We have to put a stop to this before we have any peace.'

Towser had done himself a noble job of excavation. He was almost completely out of sight. Only the end of his considerably bedraggled tail showed out of the hole he had clawed in the forest floor.

Beasly had been right about the tank-like thing. One edge of it showed out of one side of the hole.

Towser backed out of the hole and sat down heavily, his whiskers dripping clay, his tongue hanging out of the side of his mouth.

'He says that it's about time that we showed up,' said Beasly.

Taine walked around the hole and knelt down. He reached down a hand to brush the dirt off the projecting edge of Beasly's tank. The clay was stubborn and hard to wipe away, but from the feel of it the tank was heavy metal.

Taine picked up a shovel and rapped it against the tank. The tank gave out a clang.

They got to work, shovelling away a foot or so of topsoil that lay above the object. It was hard work and the thing was bigger than they had thought and it took some time to get it uncovered, even roughly.

'I'm hungry,' Beasly complained.

Taine glanced at his watch. It was almost one o'clock. 'Run on back to the house,' he said to Beasly. 'You'll find something in the refrigerator and there's milk to drink.'

'How about you, Hiram? Ain't you ever hungry?'

'You could bring me back a sandwich and see if you can find a trowel.'

'What you want a trowel for?'

'I want to scrape the dirt off this thing and see what it is.'

He squatted down beside the thing they had unearthed and watched Beasly disappear into the woods.

'Towser,' he said, 'this is the strangest animal you ever put to ground.'

A man, he told himself, might better joke about it – if to do no more than keep his fear away.

Beasly wasn't scared, of course. Beasly didn't have the sense to be scared of a thing like this.

Twelve feet wide by twenty long and oval shaped. About the size, he thought, of a good-size living-room. And there never had been a tank of that shape or size in all of Willow Bend.

He fished his jack-knife out of his pocket and started to scratch away the dirt at one point on the surface of the thing. He got a square inch free of dirt and it was no metal such as he had ever seen. It looked for all the world like glass.

He kept on scraping at the dirt until he had a clean place as big as an outstretched hand.

It wasn't any metal. He'd almost swear to that. It looked like cloudy glass – like the milk-glass goblets and bowls he was always on the look-out for. There were a lot of people who were plain nuts about it and they'd pay fancy prices for it.

He closed the knife and put it back into his pocket and

squatted, looking at the oval shape that Towser had discovered.

And the conviction grew: whatever it was that had come to live with him undoubtedly had arrived in this same contraption. From space or time, he thought, and was astonished that he thought it, for he'd never thought such a thing before.

He picked up his shovel and began to dig again, digging down this time, following the curving side of this alien thing that lay within the earth.

And as he dug, he wondered. What should he say about this – or should he say anything? Maybe the smartest course would be to cover it again and never breathe a word about it to a living soul.

Beasly would talk about it, naturally. But no one in the village would pay attention to anything that Beasly said. Everyone in Willow Bend knew Beasly was cracked.

Beasly finally came back. He carried three inexpertly-made sandwiches wrapped in an old newspaper and a quart bottle almost full of milk.

'You certainly took your time,' said Taine, slightly irritated.

'I got interested,' Beasly explained.

'Interested in what?'

'Well, there were three big trucks and they were lugging a lot of heavy stuff down into the basement. Two or three big cabinets and a lot of other junk. And you know Abbie's television set? Well, they took the set away. I told them that they shouldn't but they took it anyway.'

'I forgot,' said Taine. 'Henry said he'd send the computer over and I plumb forgot.'

Taine ate the sandwiches, sharing them with Towser, who was very grateful in a muddy way.

Finished, Taine rose and picked up his shovel.

'Let's get to work,' he said.

'But you got all that stuff down in the basement.'

'That can wait,' said Taine. 'This job we have to finish.'

It was getting dusk by the time they finished.

Taine leaned wearily on his shovel.

Twelve feet by twenty across the top and ten feet deep – and all of it, every bit of it, made of the milk-glass stuff that sounded like a bell when you whacked it with a shovel.

They'd have to be small, he thought, if there were many of them, to live in a space that size, especially if they had to stay there very long. And that fitted in, of course, for if they weren't small they couldn't now be living in the space between the basement joists.

If they were really living there, thought Taine. If it wasn't all just a lot of supposition.

Maybe, he thought, even if they had been living in the house, they might be there no longer – for Towser had smelled or heard or somehow sensed them in the morning, but by that very night he'd paid them no attention.

Taine slung his shovel across his shoulder and hoisted the pick.

'Come on,' he said, 'let's go. We've put in a long, hard day.'

They tramped out through the brush and reached the road. Fireflies were flickering off and on in the woody darkness and the street lamps were swaying in the summer breeze. The stars were hard and bright.

Maybe they still were in the house, thought Taine. Maybe when they found out that Towser had objected to them, they had fixed it so he'd be aware of them no longer.

They probably were highly adaptive. It stood to good reason they would have to be. It hadn't taken them too long, he told himself grimly, to adapt to a human house.

He and Beasly went up the gravel driveway in the dark to put the tools away in the garage and there was something funny going on, for there was no garage.

There was no garage and there was no front on the house and the driveway was cut off abruptly and there was nothing but the curving wall of what apparently had been the end of the garage.

They came up to the curving wall and stopped, squinting unbelieving in the summer dark.

There was no garage, no porch, no front of the house at all. It was as if someone had taken the opposite corners of the front of the house and bent them together until they touched, folding the entire front of the building inside the curvature of the bent-together corners.

Taine now had a curved-front house. Although it was, actually, not as simple as all that, for the curvature was not in proportion to what actually would have happened in case of such a feat. The curve was long and graceful and somehow not quite apparent. It was as if the front of the house had been eliminated and an illusion of the rest of the house had been summoned to mask the disappearance.

Taine dropped the shovel and the pick and they clattered on the driveway gravel. He put his hand up to his face and wiped it across his eyes, as if to clear his eyes of something that could not possibly be there.

And when he took the hand away it had not changed a bit.

There was no front to the house.

Then he was running around the house, hardly knowing he was running, and there was a fear inside of him at what had happened to the house.

But the back of the house was all right. It was exactly as it had always been.

He clattered up the stoop with Beasly and Towser running close behind him. He pushed open the door and burst into the entry and scrambled up the stairs into the kitchen and went across the kitchen in three strides to see what had happened to the front of the house.

At the door between the kitchen and the living-room he stopped and his hands went out to grasp the door jamb as he stared in disbelief at the windows of the living-room.

It was night outside. There could be no doubt of that. He had seen the fireflies flickering in the brush and weeds and the street lamps had been lit and the stars were out.

But a flood of sunlight was pouring through the windows of the living-room and out beyond the windows lay a land that was not Willow Bend.

'Beasly,' he gasped, 'look out there in front!'

Beasly looked.

'What place is that?' he asked.

'That's what I'd like to know.'

Towser had found his dish and was pushing it around the kitchen floor with his nose, by way of telling Taine that it was time to eat.

Taine went across the living-room and opened the front door. The garage, he saw, was there. The pick-up stood with its nose against the opening garage door and the car was safe inside.

There was nothing wrong with the front of the house at all.

But if the front of the house was all right, that was all that was.

For the driveway was chopped off just a few feet beyond the tail-end of the pick-up and there was no yard or woods or road. There was just a desert – a flat, far-reaching desert, level as a floor, with occasional boulder piles and haphazard clumps of vegetation and all of the ground covered with sand and pebbles. A big blinding sun hung just above a horizon that seemed much too far away and a funny thing about it was that the sun was in the north, where no proper sun should be. It had a peculiar whiteness, too.

Beasly stepped out on the porch and Taine saw that he was shivering like a frightened dog.

'Maybe,' Taine told him, kindly, 'you'd better go back in and start making us some supper.'

'But, Hiram – '

'It's all right,' said Taine. 'It's bound to be all right.'

'If you say so, Hiram.'

He went in and the screen door banged behind him and in a minute Taine heard him in the kitchen.

He didn't blame Beasly for shivering, he admitted to himself. It was a sort of shock to step out of your front door into an unknown land. A man might eventually get used to it, of course, but it would take some doing.

He stepped down off the porch and walked around the truck and around the garage corner and when he rounded the corner he was half prepared to walk back into familiar Willow Bend –

for when he had gone in the back door the village had been there.

There was no Willow Bend. There was more of the desert, a great deal more of it.

He walked around the house and there was no back to the house. The back of the house now was just the same as the front had been before – the same smooth curve pulling the sides of the house together.

He walked on around the house to the front again and there was desert all the way. And the front was still all right. It hadn't changed at all. The truck was there on the chopped-off driveway and the garage was open and the car inside.

Taine walked out a way into the desert and hunkered down and scooped up a handful of the pebbles and the pebbles were just pebbles.

He squatted there and let the pebbles trickle through his fingers.

In Willow Bend there was a back door and there wasn't any front. Here, wherever here might be, there was a front door, but there wasn't any back.

He stood up and tossed the rest of the pebbles away and wiped his dusty hands upon his breeches.

Out of the corner of his eye he caught a sense of movement on the porch and there they were.

A line of tiny animals, if animals they were, came marching down the steps, one behind another. They were four inches high or so and they went on all four feet, although it was plain to see that their front feet were really hands, not feet. They had rat-like faces that were vaguely human, with noses long and pointed. They looked as if they might have scales instead of hide, for their bodies glistened with a rippling motion as they walked. And all of them had tails that looked very much like the coiled-wire tails one finds on certain toys and the tails stuck straight up above them, quivering as they walked.

They came down the steps in single file, in perfect military order, with half a foot or so of spacing between each one of them.

They came down the steps and walked out into the desert in a straight, undeviating line as if they knew exactly where they might be bound. There was something deadly purposeful about them and yet they didn't hurry.

Taine counted sixteen of them and he watched them go out into the desert until they were almost lost to sight.

There go the ones, he thought, who came to live with me. They are the ones who fixed up the ceiling and who repaired Abbie's television set and jiggered up the stove and radio. And more than likely, too, they were the ones who had come to Earth in the strange milk-glass contraption out there in the woods.

And if they had come to Earth in that deal out in the woods, then what sort of place was this?

He climbed the porch and opened the screen door and saw the neat, six-inch circle his departing guests had achieved in the screen to get out of the house. He made a mental note that some day, when he had the time, he would have to fix it.

He went in and slammed the door behind him.

'Beasly,' he shouted.

There was no answer.

Towser crawled from beneath the love seat and apologized.

'It's all right, pal,' said Taine. 'That outfit scared me, too.'

He went into the kitchen. The dim ceiling light shone on the overturned coffee pot, the broken cup in the centre of the floor, the upset bowl of eggs. One broken egg was a white and yellow gob on the linoleum.

He stepped down on the landing and saw that the screen door in the back was wrecked beyond repair. Its rusty mesh was broken – exploded might have been a better word – and a part of the frame was smashed.

Taine looked at it in wondering admiration.

'The poor fool,' he said. 'He went straight through it without opening it at all.'

He snapped on the light and went down the basement stairs. Half-way down he stopped in utter wonderment.

To his left was a wall – a wall of the same sort of material as had been used to put in the ceiling.

He stooped and saw that the wall ran clear across the basement, floor to ceiling, shutting off the workshop area.

And inside the workshop, what?

For one thing, he remembered, the computer that Henry had sent over just this morning. Three trucks, Beasly had said – three truck-loads of equipment delivered straight into their paws!

Taine sat down weakly on the steps.

They must have thought, he told himself, that he was cooperating! Maybe they had figured that he knew what they were about and so went along with them. Or perhaps they thought he was paying them for fixing up the TV set and the stove and radio.

But to tackle first things first, why had they repaired the TV set and the stove and radio? As a sort of rental payment? As a friendly gesture? Or as a sort of practice run to find out what they could about this world's technology? To find, perhaps, how their technology could be adapted to the materials and conditions on this planet they had found?

Taine raised a hand and rapped with his knuckles on the wall beside the stairs and the smooth white surface gave out a pinging sound.

He laid his ear against the wall and listened closely and it seemed to him he could hear a low-key humming, but if so it was so faint he could not be absolutely sure.

Banker Stevens's lawn-mower was in there, behind the wall, and a lot of other stuff waiting for repair. They'd take the hide right off him, he thought, especially Banker Stevens. Stevens was a tight man.

Beasly must have been half-crazed with fear, he thought. When he had seen those things coming up out of the basement, he'd gone clean off his rocket. He'd gone straight through the door without even bothering to try to open it and now he was down in the village yapping to anyone who'd stop to listen to him.

No one ordinarily would pay Beasly much attention, but if

he yapped long enough and wild enough, they'd probably do some checking. They'd come storming up here and they'd give the place a going over and they'd stand goggle-eyed at what they found in front and pretty soon some of them would have worked their way around to sort of running things.

And it was none of their business, Taine stubbornly told himself, his ever-present business sense rising to the fore. There was a lot of real estate lying around out there in his front yard and the only way anyone could get to it was by going through the house. That being the case, it stood to reason that all that land out there was his. Maybe it wasn't any good at all. There might be nothing there. But before he had other people overrunning it, he'd better check and see.

He went up the stairs and out into the garage.

The sun was still just above the northern horizon and there was nothing moving.

He found a hammer and some nails and a few short lengths of plank in the garage and took them in the house.

Towser, he saw, had taken advantage of the situation and was sleeping in the gold-upholstered chair. Taine didn't bother him.

Taine locked the back door and nailed some planks across it. He locked the kitchen and the bedroom windows and nailed planks across them, too.

That would hold the villagers for a while, he told himself, when they came tearing up here to see what was going on.

He got his deer rifle, a box of cartridges, a pair of binoculars and an old canteen out of a closet. He filled the canteen at the kitchen tap and stuffed a sack with food for him and Towser to eat along the way, for there was no time to wait and eat.

Then he went into the living-room and dumped Towser out of the gold-upholstered chair.

'Come on, Tows,' he said. 'We'll go and look things over.'

He checked the gasoline in the pick-up and the tank was almost full.

He and the dog got in and he put the rifle within easy reach. Then he backed the truck and swung it around and headed out, north, across the desert.

It was easy travelling. The desert was as level as a floor. At times it got a little rough, but no worse than a lot of the back roads he travelled hunting down antiques.

The scenery didn't change. Here and there were low hills, but the desert itself kept on mostly level, unravelling itself into that far-off horizon. Taine kept on driving north, straight into the sun. He hit some sandy stretches, but the sand was firm and hard and he had no trouble.

Half an hour out he caught up with the band of things – all sixteen of them – that had left the house. They were still travelling in line at their steady pace.

Slowing down the truck, Taine travelled parallel with them for a time, but there was no profit in it; they kept on travelling their course, looking neither right nor left.

Speeding up, Taine left them behind.

The sun stayed in the north, unmoving, and that certainly was queer. Perhaps, Taine told himself, this world spun on its axis far more slowly than the Earth and the day was longer. From the way the sun appeared to be standing still, perhaps a good deal longer.

Hunched above the wheel, staring out into the endless stretch of desert, the strangeness of it struck him for the first time with its full impact.

This was another world – there could be no doubt of that – another planet circling another star, and where it was in actual space no one on Earth could have the least idea. And yet, through some machination of those sixteen things walking straight in line, it also was lying just outside the front door of his house.

Ahead of him a somewhat larger hill loomed out of the flatness of the desert. As he drew nearer to it, he made out a row of shining objects lined upon its crest. After a time he stopped the truck and got out with the binoculars.

Through the glasses, he saw that the shining things were the same sort of milk-glass contraptions as had been in the woods. He counted eight of them, shining in the sun, perched upon some sort of rock-grey cradles. And there were other cradles empty.

He took the binoculars from his eyes and stood there for a moment, considering the advisability of climbing the hill and investigating closely. But he shook his head. There'd be time for that later on. He'd better keep on moving. This was not a real exploring foray, but a quick reconnaissance.

He climbed into the truck and drove on, keeping watch upon the gas gauge. When it came close to half full he'd have to turn around and go back home again.

Ahead of him he saw a faint whiteness above the dim horizon line and he watched it narrowly. At times it faded away and then came in again, but whatever it might be was so far off he could make nothing of it.

He glanced down at the gas gauge and it was close to the half-way mark. He stopped the pick-up and got out with the binoculars.

As he moved around to the front of the machine he was puzzled at how slow and tired his legs were and then remembered – he should have been in bed many hours ago. He looked at his watch and it was two o'clock and that meant, back on Earth, two o'clock in the morning. He had been awake for more than twenty hours and much of that time he had been engaged in the back-breaking work of digging out the strange thing in the woods.

He put up the binoculars and the elusive white line that he had been seeing turned out to be a range of mountains. The great, blue, craggy mass towered up above the desert with the gleam of snow on its peaks and ridges. They were a long way off, for even the powerful glasses brought them in as little more than a misty blueness.

He swept the glasses slowly back and forth and the mountains extended for a long distance above the horizon line.

He brought the glasses down off the mountains and examined the desert that stretched ahead of him. There was more of the same that he had been seeing – the same floor-like levelness, the same occasional mounds, the self-same craggy vegetation.

And a house!

His hands trembled and he lowered the glasses, then put them up to his face again and had another look. It was a house, all right. A funny-looking house standing at the foot of one of the hillocks, still shadowed by the hillock so that one could not pick it out with the naked eye.

It seemed to be a small house. Its roof was like a blunted cone and it lay tight against the ground, as if it hugged or crouched against the ground. There was an oval opening that probably was a door, but there was no sign of windows.

He took the binoculars down again and stared at the hillock. Four or five miles away, he thought. The gas would stretch that far and even if it didn't he could walk the last few miles into Willow Bend.

It was queer, he thought, that a house should be all alone out here. In all the miles he'd travelled in the desert he'd seen no sign of life beyond the sixteen little rat-like things that marched in single file, no sign of artificial structure other than the eight milk-glass contraptions resting in their cradles.

He climbed into the pick-up and put it into gear. Ten minutes later he drew up in front of the house, which still lay within the shadow of the hillock.

He got out of the pick-up and hauled his rifle after him. Towser leaped to the ground and stood with his hackles up, a deep growl in his throat.

'What's the matter, boy?' asked Taine.

Towser growled again.

The house stood silent. It seemed to be deserted.

The walls were built, Taine saw, of rude, rough masonry, crudely set together, with a crumbling, mud-like substance used in lieu of mortar. The roof originally had been of sod and that was queer, indeed, for there was nothing that came close to sod upon this expanse of desert. But now, although one could see the lines where the sod strips had been fitted together, it was nothing more than earth baked hard by the desert sun.

The house itself was featureless, entirely devoid of any ornament, with no attempt at all to soften the harsh utility of it as a simple shelter. It was the sort of thing that a shepherd people might have put together. It had the look of age about it; the stone had flaked and crumbled in the weather.

Rifle slung beneath his arm, Taine paced towards it. He reached the door and glanced inside and there was darkness and no movement.

He glanced back for Towser and saw that the dog had crawled beneath the truck and was peering out and growling.

'You stick around,' said Taine. 'Don't go running off.'

With the rifle thrust before him, Taine stepped through the door into the darkness. He stood for a long moment to allow his eyes to become accustomed to the gloom.

Finally he could make out the room in which he stood. It was plain and rough, with a rude stone bench along one wall and queer unfunctional niches hollowed in another. One rickety piece of wooden furniture stood in a corner, but Taine could not make out what its use might be.

An old and deserted place, he thought, abandoned long ago. Perhaps a shepherd people might have lived here in some long-gone age, when the desert had been a rich and grassy plain.

There was a door into another room and as he stepped through it he heard the faint far-off booming sound and something else as well – the sound of pouring rain! From the open door that led out through the back he caught a whiff of salty breeze and he stood there frozen in the centre of that second room.

Another one!

Another house that led to another world!

He walked slowly forward, drawn towards the outer door, and he stepped out into a cloudy, darkling day with the rain steaming down from wildly racing clouds. Half a mile away, across a field of jumbled, broken, iron-grey boulders, lay a pounding sea that raged upon the coast, throwing great spumes of angry spray high into the air.

He walked out from the door and looked up at the sky, and the raindrops pounded at his face with a stinging fury. There was a chill and a dampness in the air and the place was eldritch – a world jerked straight from some ancient Gothic tale of goblin and of sprite.

He glanced around and there was nothing he could see, for the rain blotted out the world beyond this stretch of coast, but behind the rain he could sense or seemed to sense a presence that sent shivers down his spine. Gulping in fright, Taine turned around and stumbled back again through the door into the house.

One world away, he thought, was far enough; two worlds away was more than one could take. He trembled at the sense of utter loneliness that tumbled in his skull and suddenly this long-forsaken house became unbearable and he dashed out of it.

Outside the sun was bright and there was welcome warmth. His clothes were damp from rain and little beads of moisture lay on the rifle barrel.

He looked around for Towser and there was no sign of the dog. He was not underneath the pick-up; he was nowhere in sight.

Taine called and there was no answer. His voice sounded lone and hollow in the emptiness and silence.

He walked around the house, looking for the dog, and there was no back door to the house. The rough rock walls of the sides of the house pulled in with that funny curvature and there was no back to the house at all.

But Taine was not interested; he had known how it would be. Right now he was looking for his dog and he felt the panic rising in him. Somehow it felt a long way from home.

He spent three hours at it. He went back into the house and Towser was not there. He went into the other world again and searched among the tumbled rocks and Towser was not there. He went back to the desert and walked around the hillock and then he climbed to the crest of it and used the binoculars and saw nothing but the lifeless desert, stretching far in all directions.

Dead-beat with weariness, stumbling, half asleep even as he

walked, he went back to the pick-up.

He leaned against it and tried to pull his wits together.

Continuing as he was would be a useless effort. He had to get some sleep. He had to go back to Willow Bend and fill the tank and get some extra gasoline so that he could range farther afield in his search for Towser.

He couldn't leave the dog out here – that was unthinkable. But he had to plan, he had to act intelligently. He would be doing Towser no good by stumbling around in his present shape.

He pulled himself into the truck and headed back for Willow Bend, following the occasional faint impressions that his tyres had made in the sandy places, fighting a half-dead drowsiness that tried to seal his eyes shut.

Passing the higher hill on which the milk-glass things had stood, he stopped to walk around a bit so he wouldn't fall asleep behind the wheel. And now, he saw, there were only seven of the things resting in their cradles.

But that meant nothing to him now. All that meant anything was to hold off the fatigue that was closing down upon him, to cling to the wheel and wear off the miles, to get back to Willow Bend and get some sleep and then come back again to look for Towser.

Slightly more than half-way home he saw the other car and watched it in numb befuddlement, for this truck that he was driving and the car at home in his garage were the only two vehicles this side of his house.

He pulled the pick-up to a halt and tumbled out of it.

The car drew up and Henry Horton and Beasly and a man who wore a star leaped quickly out of it.

'Thank God we found you, man!' cried Henry, striding over to him.

'I wasn't lost,' protested Taine. 'I was coming back.'

'He's all beat out,' said the man who wore the star.

'This is Sheriff Hanson,' Henry said. 'We were following your tracks.'

'I lost Towser,' Taine mumbled. 'I had to go and leave

him. Just leave me be and go and hunt for Towser. I can make it home.'

He reached out and grabbed the edge of the pick-up's door to hold himself erect.

'You broke down the door,' he said to Henry. 'You broke into my house and you took my car – '

'We had to do it, Hiram. We were afraid that something might have happened to you. The way that Beasly told it, it stood your hair on end.'

'You better get him in the car,' the sheriff said. 'I'll drive the pick-up back.'

'But I have to hunt for Towser!'

'You can't do anything until you've had some rest.'

Henry grabbed him by the arm and led him to the car and Beasly held the rear door open.

'You got any idea what this place is?' Henry whispered conspiratorially.

'I don't positively know,' Taine mumbled. 'Might be some other – '

Henry chuckled. 'Well, I guess it doesn't really matter. Whatever it may be, it's put us on the map. We're in all the news-casts and the papers are plastering us in headlines and the town is swarming with reporters and cameramen and there are big officials coming. Yes, sir, I tell you, Hiram, this will be the making of us – '

Taine heard no more. He was fast asleep before he hit the seat. He came awake and lay quietly in the bed and he saw the shades were drawn and the room was cool and peaceful.

It was good, he thought, to wake in a room you knew – in a room that one had known for one's entire life, in a house that had been the Taine house for almost a hundred years.

Then memory clouted him and he sat bolt upright.

And now he heard it – the insistent murmur from outside the window.

He vaulted from the bed and pulled one shade aside. Peering out, he saw the cordon of troops that held back the crowd that overflowed his back yard and the back yards back of that.

He let the shade drop back and started hunting for his shoes, for he was fully dressed. Probably Henry and Beasly, he told himself, had dumped him into bed and pulled off his shoes and let it go at that. But he couldn't remember a single thing of it. He must have gone dead to the world the minute Henry had bundled him into the back seat of the car.

He found the shoes on the floor at the end of the bed and sat down upon the bed to pull them on.

And his mind was racing on what he had to do.

He'd have to get some gasoline somehow and fill up the truck and stash an extra can or two into the back and he'd have to take some food and water and perhaps his sleeping-bag. For he wasn't coming back until he found his dog.

He got on his shoes and tied them, then went out into the living-room. There was no one there, but there were voices in the kitchen.

He looked out of the window and the desert lay outside, unchanged. The sun, he noticed, had climbed higher in the sky, but out in his front yard it was still forenoon.

He looked at his watch and it was six o'clock and from the way the shadows had been falling when he'd peered out of the bedroom window, he knew that it was 6 p.m. He realized with a guilty start that he must have slept almost around the clock. He had not meant to sleep that long. He hadn't meant to leave Towser out there that long.

He headed for the kitchen and there were three persons there – Abbie and Henry Horton and a man in military garb.

'There you are,' cried Abbie merrily. 'We were wondering when you would wake up.'

'You have some coffee cooking, Abbie?'

'Yes, a whole pot full of it. And I'll cook up something else for you.'

'Just some toast,' said Taine. 'I haven't got much time. I have to hunt for Towser.'

'Hiram,' said Henry, 'this is Colonel Ryan, National Guard. He has his boys outside.'

'Yes, I saw them through the window.'

'Necessary,' said Henry. 'Absolutely necessary. The sheriff couldn't handle it. The people came rushing in and they'd have torn the place apart. So I called the governor.'

'Taine,' the colonel said, 'sit down. I want to talk with you.'

'Certainly,' said Taine, taking a chair. 'Sorry to be in such a rush, but I lost my dog out there.'

'This business,' said the colonel, smugly, 'is vastly more important than any dog could be.'

'Well, colonel, that just goes to show that you don't know Towser. He's the best dog I ever had and I've had a lot of them. Raised him from a pup and he's been a good friend all these years – '

'All right,' the colonel said, 'so he is a friend. But still I have to talk with you.'

'You just sit and talk,' Abbie said to Taine. 'I'll fix up some cakes and Henry brought over some of that sausage that we get out on the farm.'

The back door opened and Beasly staggered in to the accompaniment of a terrific metallic banging. He was carrying three empty five-gallon gas cans in one hand and two in the other hand and they were bumping and banging together as he moved.

'Say,' yelled Taine, 'what's going on here?'

'Now, just take it easy,' Henry said. 'You have no idea the problems that we have. We wanted to get a big gas tank moved through here, but we couldn't do it. We tried to rip out the back of the kitchen to get it through, but we couldn't – '

'You did what!'

'We tried to rip out the back of the kitchen,' Henry told him calmly. 'You can't get one of those big storage tanks through an ordinary door. But when we tried, we found that the entire house is boarded up inside with the same kind of material that you used down in the basement. You hit it with an axe and it blunts the steel – '

'But, Henry, this is my house and there isn't anyone who has the right to start tearing it apart.'

'Fat chance,' the colonel said. 'What I would like to know,

Taine, what is that stuff that we couldn't break through?'

'Now you take it easy, Hiram,' cautioned Henry. 'We have a big new world waiting for us out there – '

'It isn't waiting for you or anyone,' yelled Taine.

'And we have to explore it and to explore it we need a stockpile of gasoline. So since we can't have a storage tank, we're getting together as many gas cans as possible and then we'll run a hose through here – '

'But, Henry – '

'I wish,' said Henry sternly, 'that you'd quit interrupting me and let me have my say. You can't even imagine the logistics that we face. We're bottle-necked by the size of a regulation door. We have to get supplies out there and we have to get transport. Cars and trucks won't be so bad. We can disassemble them and lug them through piecemeal, but a plane will be a problem.'

'You listen to me, Henry. There isn't anyone going to haul a plane through here. This house has been in my family for almost a hundred years and I own it and I have a right to it and you can't come in high-handed and start hauling stuff through it.'

'But,' said Henry plaintively, 'we need a plane real bad. You can cover so much more ground when you have a plane.'

Beasly went banging through the kitchen with his cans and out into the living-room.

The colonel sighed. 'I had hoped, Mr Taine, that you would understand how the matter stood. To me it seems very plain that it's your patriotic duty to co-operate with us in this. The government, of course, could exercise the right of eminent domain and start condemnation action, but it would rather not do that. I'm speaking unofficially, of course, but I think it's safe to say the government would much prefer to arrive at an amicable agreement.'

'I doubt,' Taine said, bluffing, not knowing anything about it, 'that the right to eminent domain would be applicable. As I understand it, it applies to buildings and to roads – '

'This is a road,' the colonel told him flatly. 'A road right through your house to another world.'

'First,' Taine declared, 'the government would have to show it was in the public interest and that refusal of the owner to relinquish title amounted to an interference in government procedure and – '

'I think,' the colonel said, 'that the government can prove it is in the public interest.'

'I think,' Taine said angrily, 'I better get a lawyer.'

'If you really mean that,' Henry offered, ever helpful, 'and you want a good one – and I presume you do – I would be pleased to recommend a firm that I am sure would represent your interests most ably and be, at the same time, fairly reasonable in cost.'

The colonel stood up, seething. 'You'll have a lot to answer, Taine. There'll be a lot of things the government will want to know. First of all, they'll want to know just how you engineered this. Are you ready to tell that?'

'No,' said Taine, 'I don't believe I am.'

And he thought with some alarm: They think that I'm the one who did it and they'll be down on me like a pack of wolves to find out just how I did it. He had visions of the FBI and the state department and the Pentagon and, even sitting down, he felt shaky in the knees.

The colonel turned around and marched stiffly from the kitchen. He went out the back and slammed the door behind him.

Henry looked at Taine speculatively.

'Do you really mean it?' he demanded. 'Do you intend to stand up to them?'

'I'm getting sore,' said Taine. 'They can't come in here and take over without even asking me. I don't care what anyone may think, this is my house. I was born here and I've lived here all my life and I like the place and – '

'Sure,' said Henry. 'I know just how you feel.'

'I suppose it's childish of me, but I wouldn't mind so much if they showed a willingness to sit down and talk about what they meant to do once they'd taken over. But there seems no disposition to even ask me what I think about it. And I tell you, Henry, this is different than it seems. This isn't a place where we can walk in and take over, no matter what Washington may think. There's something out there and we better watch our step – '

'I was thinking,' Henry interrupted, 'as I was sitting here, that your attitude is most commendable and deserving of support. It has occurred to me that it would be most unneighbourly of me to go on sitting here and leave you in the fight alone. We could hire ourselves a fine array of legal talent and we could fight the case and in the meantime we could form a land and development company and that way we could make sure that this new world of yours is used the way it should be used.

'It stands to reason, Hiram, that I am the one to stand beside you, shoulder to shoulder, in this business since we're already partners in this TV deal.'

'What's this about TV?' shrilled Abbie, slapping a plate of cakes down in front of Taine.

'Now, Abbie,' Henry said patiently, 'I have explained to you already that your TV set is back of that partition down in the basement and there isn't any telling when we can get it out.'

'Yes, I know,' said Abbie, bringing a platter of sausages and pouring a cup of coffee.

Beasly came in from the living-room and went bumbling out the back.

'After all,' said Henry, pressing his advantage, 'I would suppose I had some hand in it. I doubt you could have done much without the computer I sent over.'

And there it was again, thought Taine. Even Henry thought he'd been the one who did it.

'But didn't Beasly tell you?'

'Beasly said a lot, but you know how Beasly is.'

And that was it, of course. To the villagers it would be no more than another Beasly story – another whopper that Beasly had dreamed up. There was no one who believed a word that Beasly said.

Taine picked up the cup and drank his coffee, gaining time to shape an answer and there wasn't any answer. If he told the truth, it would sound far less believable than any lie he'd tell.

'You can tell me, Hiram. After all, we're partners.'

He's playing me for a fool, thought Taine. Henry thinks he can play anyone he wants for a fool and sucker.

'You wouldn't believe me if I told you, Henry.'

'Well,' Henry said, resignedly, getting to his feet, 'I guess that part of it can wait.'

Beasly came tramping and banging through the kitchen with another load of cans.

'I'll have to have some gasoline,' said Taine, 'if I'm going out for Towser.'

'I'll take care of that right away,' Henry promised smoothly. 'I'll send Ernie over with his tank-wagon and we can run a hose through here and fill up those cans. And I'll see if I can find someone who'll go along with you.'

'That's not necessary. I can go alone.'

'If we had a radio transmitter. Then you could keep in touch.'

'But we haven't any. And, Henry, I can't wait. Towser's out there somewhere – '

'Sure, I know how much you thought of him. You go out and look for him if you think you have to and I'll get started on this other business. I'll get some lawyers lined up and we'll draw up some sort of corporate papers for our land development – '

'And, Hiram,' Abbie said, 'will you do something for me, please?'

'Why, certainly,' said Taine.

'Would you speak to Beasly? It's senseless the way he's acting. There wasn't any call for him to up and leave us. I might have been a little sharp with him, but he's so simple-minded he's infuriating. He ran off and spent half a day helping Towser at digging out that woodchuck and – '

'I'll speak to him,' said Taine.

'Thanks, Hiram. He'll listen to you. You're the only one

he'll listen to. And I wish you could have fixed my TV set before all this came about. I'm just lost without it. It leaves a hole in the living-room. It matched my other furniture, you know.'

'Yes I know,' said Taine.

'Coming, Abbie?' Henry asked, standing at the door.

He lifted a hand in a confidential farewell to Taine. 'I'll see you later, Hiram. I'll get it all fixed up.'

I just bet you will, thought Taine.

He went back to the table, after they were gone, and sat down heavily in a chair.

The front door slammed and Beasly came panting in, excited.

'Towser's back!' he yelled. 'He's coming back and he's driving in the biggest woodchuck you ever clapped your eyes on.'

Taine leaped to his feet.

'Woodchuck! That's an alien planet. It hasn't any woodchucks.'

'You come and see,' yelled Beasly.

He turned and raced back out again, with Taine following close behind.

It certainly looked considerably like a woodchuck – a sort of man-size woodchuck. More like a woodchuck out of a children's book, perhaps, for it was walking on its hind legs and trying to look dignified even while it kept a weather eye on Towser.

Towser was back a hundred feet or so, keeping a wary distance from the massive chuck. He had the pose of a good sheep-herding dog, walking in a crouch, alert to head off any break that the chuck might make.

The chuck came up close to the house and stopped. Then it did an about-face so that it looked back across the desert and it hunkered down.

It swung its massive head to gaze at Beasly and Taine and in the limpid brown eyes Taine saw more than the eyes of an animal.

Taine walked swiftly out and picked up the dog in his arms and hugged him tight against him. Towser twisted his head around and slapped a sloppy tongue across his master's face.

Taine stood with the dog in his arms and looked at the man-size chuck and felt a great relief and an utter thankfulness.

Everything was all right now, he thought. Towser had come back.

He headed for the house and out into the kitchen.

He put Towser down and got a dish and filled it at the tap. He placed it on the floor and Towser lapped at it thirstily, slopping water all over the linoleum.

'Take it easy, there,' warned Taine. 'You don't want to overdo it.'

He hunted in the refrigerator and found some scraps and put them in Towser's dish.

Towser wagged his tail with doggish happiness.

'By rights,' said Taine, 'I ought to take a rope to you, running off like that.'

Beasly came ambling in.

'That chuck is a friendly cuss,' he announced. 'He's waiting for someone.'

'That's nice.' said Taine, paying no attention.

He glanced at the clock.

'It's seven-thirty,' he said. 'We can catch the news. You want to get it, Beasly?'

'Sure. I know right where to get it. That fellow from New York.'

'That's the one,' said Taine.

He walked into the living-room and looked out of the window. The man-size chuck had not moved. He was sitting with his back to the house, looking back the way he'd come.

Waiting for someone, Beasly had said, and it looked as if he might be, but probably it was all just in Beasly's head.

And if he were waiting for someone, Taine wondered, who might that someone be? Certainly by now the word had spread out that there was a door into another world. And how many doors, he wondered, had been opened through the ages?

Henry had said that there was a big new world out there waiting for Earthmen to move in. And that wasn't it at all. It was the other way around.

The voice of the news commentator came blasting from the radio in the middle of a sentence:

'. . . finally got into the act. Radio Moscow said this evening that the Soviet delegate will make representations in the UN tomorrow for the internationalization of this other world and the gateway to it.

'From that gateway itself, the home of a man named Hiram Taine, there is no news. Complete security has been clamped down and a cordon of troops form a solid wall around the house, holding back the crowds. Attempts to telephone the residence are blocked by a curt voice which says that no calls are being accepted for that number. And Taine himself has not stepped from the house.'

Taine walked back into the kitchen and sat down.

'He's talking about you,' Beasly said importantly.

'Rumour circulated this morning that Taine, a quiet village repair man and dealer in antiques, and until yesterday a relative unknown, had finally returned from a trip which he made out into this new and unknown land. But what he found, if anything, no one yet can say. Nor is there any further information about this other place beyond the fact that it is a desert and, to the moment, lifeless.

'A small flurry of excitement was occasioned late yesterday by the finding of some strange object in the woods across the road from the residence, but this area likewise was swiftly cordoned off and to the moment Colonel Ryan, who commands the troops, will say nothing of what actually was found.

'Mystery man of the entire situation is one Henry Horton, who seems to be the only unofficial person to have entry to the Taine house. Horton, questioned earlier today, had little to say, but managed to suggest an air of great conspiracy. He hinted he and Taine were partners in some mysterious venture and left hanging in mid air the half impression that he and Taine had collaborated in opening the new world.

'Horton, it is interesting to note, operates a small computer plant and it is understood on good authority that only recently he delivered a computer to Taine, or at least some sort of machine to which considerable mystery is attached. One story is that this particular machine had been in the process of development for six or seven years.

'Some of the answers to the matter of how all this did happen and what actually did happen must wait upon the findings of a team of scientists who left Washington this evening after an all-day conference at the White House, which was attended by representatives from the military, the state department, the security division and the special weapons section.

'Throughout the world the impact of what happened yesterday at Willow Bend can only be compared to the sensation of the news, almost twenty years ago, of the dropping of the first atomic bomb. There is some tendency among many observers to believe that the implications of Willow Bend, in fact, may be even more earth-shaking than were those at Hiroshima.

'Washington insists, as is only natural, that this matter is of internal concern only and that it intends to handle the situation as it best affects the national welfare.

'But abroad there is a rising storm of insistence that this is not a matter of national policy concerning one nation, but that it necessarily must be a matter of worldwide concern.

'There is an unconfirmed report that a UN observer will arrive in Willow Bend almost momentarily. France, Britain, Bolivia, Mexico and India have already requested permission of Washington to send observers to the scene and other nations undoubtedly plan to file similar requests.

'The world sits on edge tonight, waiting for the word from Willow Bend and – '

Taine reached out and clicked the radio to silence.

'From the sound of it,' said Beasly, 'we're going to be overrun by a batch of foreigners.'

Yes, thought Taine, there might be a batch of foreigners, but not exactly in the sense that Beasly meant. The use of the word, he told himself, so far as any human was concerned, must be outdated now. No man of Earth ever again could be called a foreigner with alien life next door – literally next door. What were the people of the stone house?

And perhaps not the alien life of one planet only, but the alien life of many. For he himself had found another door into yet another planet and there might be many more such doors and what would these other worlds be like, and what was the purpose of the doors?

Someone, *something*, had found a way of going to another planet short of spanning light-years of lonely space – a simpler and a shorter way than flying through the gulfs of space. And once the way was open, then the way stayed open and it was as easy as walking from one room to another.

But one thing – one ridiculous thing – kept puzzling him and that was the spinning and the movement of the connected planets, of all the planets that must be linked together. You could not, he argued, establish solid, factual links between two objects that move independently of one another.

And yet, a couple of days ago, he would have contended just as stolidly that the whole idea on the face of it was fantastic and impossible. Still it had been done. And once one impossibility was accomplished, what logical man could say with sincerity that the second could not be?

The doorbell rang and he got up to answer it.

It was Ernie, the oilman.

'Henry said you wanted some gas and I came to tell you I can't get it until morning.'

'That's all right,' said Taine. 'I don't need it now.'

And swiftly slammed the door.

He leaned against it, thinking: 'I'll have to face them some time. I can't keep the door locked against the world. Some time, soon or late, the Earth and I will have to have this out.'

And it was foolish, he thought, for him to think like this, but that was the way it was.

He had something here that the Earth demanded; something that Earth wanted or thought it wanted. And yet, in the last analysis, it was his responsibility. It had happened on his land, it had happened in his house; unwittingly, perhaps, he'd even aided and abetted it.

And the land and house are mine, he fiercely told himself, and that world out there was an extension of his yard. No matter how far or where it went, an extension of his yard.

Beasly had left the kitchen and Taine walked into the living-room. Towser was curled up and snoring gently in the gold-upholstered chair.

Taine decided he would let him stay there. After all, he thought, Towser had won the right to sleep anywhere he wished.

He walked past the chair to the window and the desert stretched to its far horizon and there before the window sat the man-size woodchuck and Beasly side by side, with their backs turned to the window and staring out across the desert.

Somehow it seemed natural that the chuck and Beasly should be sitting there together – the two of them, it appeared to Taine, might have a lot in common.

And it was a good beginning – that a man and an alien creature from this other world should sit down companionably together.

He tried to envision the set-up of these linked worlds, of which Earth was now a part, and the possibilities that lay inherent in the fact of linkage rolled thunder through his brain.

There would be contact between the Earth and these other worlds and what would come of it?

And come to think of it, the contact had been made already, but so naturally, so undramatically, that it failed to register as a great, important meeting. For Beasly and the chuck out there were contact and if it all should go like that, there was absolutely nothing for one to worry over.

This was no haphazard business, he reminded himself. It had been planned and executed with the smoothness of long practice. This was not the first world to be opened and it would not be the last.

The little rat-like things had spanned space – how many

light-years of space one could not even guess – in the vehicle which he had unearthed out in the woods. They then had buried it, perhaps as a child might hide a dish by shoving it into a pile of sand. Then they had come to this very house and had set up the apparatus that had made this house a tunnel between one world and another. And once that had been done, the need of crossing space had been cancelled out for ever. There need be but one crossing and that one crossing would serve to link the planets.

And once the job was done the little rat-like things had left, but not before they had made certain that this gateway to their planet would stand against no matter what assault. They had sheathed the house inside the studdings with a wonder-material that would resist an axe and that, undoubtedly, would resist much more than a simple axe.

And they had marched in drill-order single file out to the hill where eight more of the space machines had rested in their cradles. And now there were only seven there, in their cradles on the hill, and the rat-like things were gone and, perhaps, in time to come, they'd land on another planet and another doorway would be opened, a link to yet another world.

But more, Taine thought, than the linking of mere worlds. It would be, as well, the linking of the peoples of those worlds.

The little rat-like creatures were the explorers and the pioneers who sought out other Earth-like planets and the creature waiting with Beasly just outside the window must also serve its purpose and perhaps in time to come there would be a purpose which man would also serve.

He turned away from the window and looked around the room and the room was exactly as it had been ever since he could remember it. With all the change outside, with all that was happening outside, the room remained unchanged.

This is the reality, thought Taine, this is all the reality there is. Whatever else may happen, this is where I stand – this room with its fireplace blackened by many winter fires, the bookshelves with the old thumbed volumes, the easy-chair, the ancient worn carpet – worn by beloved and unforgotten feet through the many years.

And this also, he knew, was the lull before the storm.

In just a little while the brass would start arriving – the team of scientists, the governmental functionaries, the military, the observers from the other countries, the officials from the UN.

And against all these, he realized, he stood weaponless and shorn of his strength. No matter what a man might say or think, he could not stand off the world.

This was the last day that this would be the Taine house. After almost a hundred years, it would have another destiny.

And for the first time in all those years there'd be no Taine asleep beneath its roof.

He stood looking at the fireplace and the shelves of books and he sensed the old, pale ghosts walking in the room and he lifted a hesitant hand as if to wave farewell, not only to the ghosts but to the room as well. But before he got it up, he dropped it to his side.

What was the use, he thought.

He went out to the porch and sat down on the steps.

Beasly heard him and turned around.

'He's nice,' he said to Taine, patting the chuck upon the back. 'He's exactly like a great big Teddy bear.'

'Yes, I see,' said Taine.

'And best of all, I can talk with him.'

'Yes, I know,' said Taine, remembering that Beasly could talk with Towser, too.

He wondered what it would be like to live in the simple world of Beasly. At times, he decided, it would be comfortable.

The rat-like things had come in the spaceship, but why had they come to Willow Bend, why had they picked this house, the only house in all the village where they would have found the equipment that they needed to build their apparatus so easily and so quickly? For there was no doubt that they had cannibalized the computer to get the equipment they needed. In that, at least, Henry had been right. Thinking back on it, Henry, after all, had played quite a part in it.

Could they have foreseen that on this particular week in this particular house the probability of quickly and easily doing what they had come to do had stood very high?

Did they, with all their other talents and technology, have clairvoyance as well?

'There's someone coming,' Beasly said.

'I don't see a thing.'

'Neither do I,' said Beasly, 'but Chuck told me that he saw them.'

'Told you!'

'I told you we been talking. There, I can see them too.'

They were far off, but they were coming fast – three dots rode rapidly out of the desert.

He sat and watched them come and he thought of going in to get the rifle, but he didn't stir from his seat upon the steps. The rifle would do no good, he told himself. It would be a senseless thing to get it; more than that, a senseless attitude. The least that man could do, he thought, was to meet these creatures of another world with clean and empty hands.

They were closer now and it seemed to him that they were sitting in invisible chairs that travelled very fast.

He saw that they were humanoid, to a degree at least, and there were only three of them.

They came in with a rush and stopped very suddenly a hundred feet or so from where he sat upon the steps.

He didn't move or say a word – there was nothing he could say. It was too ridiculous.

They were, perhaps, a little smaller than himself, and black as the ace of spades, and they wore skin-tight shorts and vests that were somewhat oversize and both the shorts and vests were the blue of April skies.

But that was not the worst of it.

They sat on saddles, with horns in front and stirrups and a sort of bedroll tied on the back, but they had no horses.

The saddles floated in the air, with the stirrups about three feet above the ground and the aliens sat easily in the saddles and stared at him and he stared back at them.

Finally he got up and moved forward a step or two and when

he did that the three swung from the saddles and moved forward, too, while the saddles hung there in the air, exactly as they'd left them.

Taine walked forward and the three walked forward until they were no more than six feet apart.

'They say hello to you,' said Beasly. 'They say welcome to you.'

'Well, all right, then, tell them – Say, how do you know all this?'

'Chuck tells me what they say and I tell you. You tell me and I tell him and he tells them. That's the way it works. That is what he's here for.'

'Well, I'll be – ' said Taine. 'So you can really talk to him.'

'I told you that I could,' stormed Beasly. 'I told you that I could talk to Towser, too, but you thought that I was crazy.'

'Telepathy!' said Taine. And it was worse than ever now. Not only had the rat-like things known all the rest of it, but they'd known of Beasly, too.

'What was that you said, Hiram?'

'Never mind,' said Taine. 'Tell that friend of yours to tell them I'm glad to meet them and what can I do for them?'

He stood uncomfortably and stared at the three and he saw that their vests had many pockets and that the pockets were crammed, probably with their equivalent of tobacco and handkerchiefs and pocket knives and such.

'They say,' said Beasly, 'that they want to dicker.'

'Dicker?'

'Sure, Hiram. You know, trade.'

Beasly chuckled thinly. 'Imagine them laying themselves open to a Yankee trader. That's what Henry says you are. He says you can skin a man on the slickest – '

'Leave Henry out of this,' snapped Taine. 'Let's leave Henry out of something.'

He sat down on the ground and the three sat down to face him.

'Ask them what they have in mind to trade.'

'Ideas,' Beasly said.

'Ideas! That's a crazy thing – '

And then he saw it wasn't.

Of all the commodities that might be exchanged by an alien people, ideas would be the most valuable and the easiest to handle. They'd take no cargo room and they'd upset no economies – not immediately, that is – and they'd make a bigger contribution to the welfare of the cultures than trade in actual goods.

'Ask them,' said Taine, 'what they'll take for the idea back of those saddles they are riding.'

'They say, what have you to offer?'

And that was the stumper. That was the one that would be hard to answer.

Automobiles and trucks, the internal gas engine – well, probably not. Because they already had the saddles. Earth was out of date in transportation from the viewpoint of these people.

Housing architecture – no, that was hardly an idea and, anyhow, there was that other house, so they knew of houses.

Cloth? No, they had cloth.

Paint, he thought. Maybe paint was it.

'See if they are interested in paint,' Taine told Beasly.

'They say, what is it? Please explain yourself.'

'OK, then. Let's see. It's a protective device to be spread over almost any surface. Easily packaged and easily applied. Protects against weather and corrosion. It's decorative, too. Comes in all sorts of colours. And it's cheap to make.'

'They shrug in their mind,' said Beasly. 'They're just slightly interested. But they'll listen more. Go ahead and tell them.'

And that was more like it, thought Taine.

That was the kind of language that he could understand.

He settled himself more firmly on the ground and bent forward slightly, flicking his eyes across the three dead-pan, ebony faces, trying to make out what they might be thinking.

There was no making out. Those were three of the deadest pans he had ever seen.

It was all familiar. It made him feel at home. He was in his element.

And in the three across from him, he felt somehow subconsciously, he had the best dickering opposition he had ever met. And that made him feel good too.

'Tell them,' he said, 'that I'm not quite sure. I may have spoken up too hastily. Paint, after all, is a mighty valuable idea.'

'They say, just as a favour to them, not that they're really interested, would you tell them a little more.'

Got them hooked, Taine told himself. If he could only play it right –

He settled down to dickering in earnest.

Hours later Henry Horton showed up. He was accompanied by a very urbane gentleman, who was faultlessly turned out and who carried beneath his arm an impressive attaché case.

Henry and the man stopped on the steps in sheer astonishment.

Taine was squatted on the ground with a length of board and he was daubing paint on it while the aliens watched. From the daubs here and there upon their anatomies, it was plain to see the aliens had been doing some daubing of their own. Spread all over the ground were other lengths of half-painted boards and a couple of dozen old cans of paint.

Taine looked up and saw Henry and the man.

'I was hoping,' he said, 'that someone would show up.'

'Hiram,' said Henry, with more importance than usual, 'may I present Mr Lancaster. He is a special representative of the United Nations.'

'I'm glad to meet you, sir,' said Taine. 'I wonder if you would – '

'Mr Lancaster,' Henry explained grandly, 'was having some slight difficulty getting through the lines outside, so I volunteered my services. I've already explained to him our joint interest in this matter.'

'It was very kind of Mr Horton,' Lancaster said. 'There was

this stupid sergeant – '

'It's all in knowing,' Henry said, 'how to handle people.'

The remark, Taine noticed, was not appreciated by the man from the UN.

'May I inquire, Mr Taine,' asked Lancaster, 'exactly what you're doing?'

'I'm dickering,' said Taine.

'Dickering. What a quaint way of expressing – '

'An old Yankee word,' said Henry quickly, 'with certain connotations of its own. When you trade with someone you are exchanging goods, but if you're dickering with him you're out to get his hide.'

'Interesting,' said Lancaster. 'And I suppose you're out to skin these gentlemen in the sky-blue vests – '

'Hiram,' said Henry, proudly, 'is the sharpest dickerer in these parts. He runs an antique business and he has to dicker hard – '

'And may I ask,' said Lancaster, ignoring Henry finally, 'what you might be doing with these cans of paint? Are these gentlemen potential customers for paint or – '

Taine threw down the board and rose angrily to his feet.

'If you'd both shut up!' he shouted. 'I've been trying to say something ever since you got here and I can't get in a word. And I tell you, it's important – '

'Hiram!' Henry exclaimed in horror.

'It's quite all right,' said the UN man. 'We *have* been jabbering. And now, Mr Taine?'

'I'm backed into a corner,' Taine told him, 'and I need some help. I've sold these fellows on the idea of paint, but I don't know a thing about it – the principle back of it or how it's made or what goes into it or – '

'But, Mr Taine, if you're selling them the paint, what difference does it make – '

'I'm not selling them the paint,' yelled Taine. 'Can't you understand that? They don't want the paint. They want the *idea* of paint, the principle of paint. It's something that they never thought of and they're interested. I offered them the paint idea for the idea of their saddles and I've almost got it – '

'Saddles? You mean those things over there, hanging in the air?'

'That is right. Beasly, would you ask one of our friends to demonstrate a saddle?'

'You bet I will,' said Beasly.

'What,' demanded Henry, 'has Beasly got to do with this?'

'Beasly is an interpreter. I guess you'd call him a telepath. You remember how he always claimed he could talk with Towser?'

'Beasly was always claiming things.'

'But this time he was right. He tells Chuck, that funny-looking monster, what I want to say and Chuck tells these aliens. And these aliens tell Chuck and Chuck tells Beasly and Beasly tells me.'

'Ridiculous!' snorted Henry. 'Beasly hasn't got the sense to be . . . what did you say he was?'

'A telepath,' said Taine.

One of the aliens had gotten up and climbed into a saddle. He rode it forth and back. Then he swung out of it and sat down again.

'Remarkable,' said the UN man. 'Some sort of anti-gravity unit, with complete control. We could make use of that, indeed.'

He scraped his hand across his chin.

'And you're going to exchange the idea of paint for the idea of that saddle?'

'That's exactly it,' said Taine, 'but I need some help. I need a chemist or a paint manufacturer or someone to explain how paint is made. And I need some professor or other who'll understand what they're talking about when they tell me the idea of the saddle.'

'I see,' said Lancaster. 'Yes, indeed, you have a problem. Mr Taine, you seem to me a man of some discernment – '

'Oh, he's all of that,' interrupted Henry. 'Hiram's quite astute.'

'So I suppose you'll understand,' said the UN man, 'that

this whole procedure is quite irregular – '

'But it's not,' exploded Taine. 'That's the way they operate. They open up a planet and then they exchange ideas. They've been doing that with other planets for a long, long time. And ideas are all they want, just the new ideas, because that is the way to keep on building a technology and culture. And they have a lot of ideas, sir, that the human race can use.'

'That is just the point,' said Lancaster. 'This is perhaps the most important thing that has ever happened to us humans. In just a short year's time we can obtain data and ideas that will put us ahead – theoretically, at least – by a thousand years. And in a thing that is so important, we should have experts on the job – '

'But,' protested Henry, 'you can't find a man who'll do a better dickering job than Hiram. When you dicker with him your back teeth aren't safe. Why don't you leave him be? He'll do a job for you. You can get your experts and your planning groups together and let Hiram front for you. These folks have accepted him and have proved they'll do business with him and what more do you want? All he needs is a little help.'

Beasly came over and faced the UN man.

'I won't work with no one else,' he said. 'If you kick Hiram out of here, then I go with him. Hiram's the only person who ever treated me like a human – '

'There, you see!' Henry said, triumphantly.

'Now, wait a second, Beasly,' said the UN man. 'We could make it worth your while. I should imagine that an interpreter in a situation such as this could command a handsome salary.'

'Money don't mean a thing to me,' said Beasly. 'It won't buy me friends. People will still laugh at me.'

'He means it, mister,' Henry warned. 'There isn't anyone who can be as stubborn as Beasly. I know; he used to work for us.'

The UN man looked flabbergasted and not a little desperate.

'It will take you quite some time,' Henry pointed out, 'to find another telepath – leastwise one who can talk to these people here.'

The UN man looked as if he were strangling. 'I doubt,' he said, 'there's another one on Earth.'

'Well, all right,' said Beasly, brutally. 'let's make up our minds. I ain't standing here all day.'

'All right,' cried the UN man. 'You two go ahead. Please, will you go ahead? This is a chance we can't let slip through our fingers. Is there anything you want? Anything I can do for you?'

'Yes, there is,' said Taine. 'There'll be the boys from Washington and bigwigs from other countries. Just keep them off my back.'

'I'll explain most carefully to everyone. There'll be no interference.'

'And I need that chemist and someone who'll know about the saddles. And I need them quick. I can stall these boys a little longer, but not for too much longer.'

'Anyone you need,' said the UN man. 'Anyone at all. I'll have them here in hours. And in a day or two there'll be a pool of experts waiting for whenever you may need them – on a moment's notice.'

'Sir,' said Henry, unctuously, 'that's most co-operative. Both Hiram and I appreciate it greatly. And now, since this is settled, I understand that there are reporters waiting. They'll be interested in your statement.'

The UN man, it seemed, didn't have it in him to protest. He and Henry went tramping up the stairs.

Taine turned around and looked out across the desert.

'It's a big front yard,' he said.

A MEETING WITH MEDUSA

By Arthur C. Clarke

1. A DAY TO REMEMBER

The *Queen Elizabeth* was over three miles above the Grand Canyon, dawdling along at a comfortable hundred and eighty, when Howard Falcon spotted the camera platform closing in from the right. He had been expecting it – nothing else was cleared to fly at this altitude – but he was not too happy to have company. Although he welcomed any signs of public interest, he also wanted as much empty sky as he could get. After all, he was the first man in history to navigate a ship three-tenths of a mile long . . .

So far, this first test flight had gone perfectly; ironically enough, the only problem had been the century-old aircraft carrier *Chairman Mao*, borrowed from the San Diego Naval Museum for support operations. Only one of *Mao*'s four nuclear reactors was still operating, and the old battlewagon's top speed was barely thirty knots. Luckily, wind speed at sea level had been less than half this, so it had not been too difficult to maintain this still air on the flight deck. Though there had been a few anxious moments during gusts, when the mooring lines had been dropped, the great dirigible had risen smoothly, straight up into the sky, as if on an invisible elevator. If all went well, *Queen Elizabeth IV* would not meet *Chairman Mao* again for another week.

Everything was under control; all test instruments gave normal readings. Commander Falcon decided to go upstairs and watch the rendezvous. He handed over to his second officer, and walked out into the transparent tubeway that led through the heart of the ship. There, as always, he was overwhelmed by the spectacle of the largest single space ever enclosed by man.

The ten spherical gas cells, each more than a hundred feet across, were ranged one behind the other like a line of gigantic soap bubbles. The tough plastic was so clear that he could see through the whole length of the array, and make out details of the elevator mechanism, more than a third of a mile from his vantage point. All around him, like a three-dimensional maze, was the structural framework of the ship – the great longitudinal girders running from nose to tail, the fifteen hoops that were the circular ribs of this sky-borne colossus, and whose varying sizes defined its graceful, streamlined profile.

At this low speed, there was little sound – merely the soft rush of wind over the envelope and an occasional creak of metal as the pattern of stresses changed. The shadowless light from the rows of lamps far overhead gave the whole scene a curiously submarine quality, and to Falcon this was enhanced by the spectacle of the translucent gasbags. He had once encountered a squadron of large but harmless jellyfish, pulsing their mindless way above a shallow tropical reef, and the plastic bubbles that gave *Queen Elizabeth* her lift often reminded him of these – especially when changing pressures made them crinkle and scatter new patterns of reflected light.

He walked down the axis of the ship until he came to the forward elevator, between gas cells one and two. Riding up to the Observation Deck, he noticed that it was uncomfortably hot, and dictated a brief memo to himself on his pocket recorder. The *Queen* obtained almost a quarter of her buoyancy from the unlimited amounts of waste heat produced by her fusion power plant. On this lightly loaded flight, indeed, only six of the ten gas cells contained helium; the remaining four were full of air. Yet she still carried two hundred tons of water as ballast. However, running the cells at high temperatures did produce problems in refrigerating the access ways; it was obvious that a little more work would have to be done there.

A refreshing blast of cooler air hit him in the face when he stepped out on to the Observation Deck and into the dazzling sunlight streaming through the plexiglass roof. Half a dozen workmen, with an equal number of superchimp assistants, were busily laying the partly completed dance floor, while others were installing electric wiring and fixing furniture. It was a scene of controlled chaos, and Falcon found it hard to believe that everything would be ready for the maiden voyage, only four weeks ahead. Well, that was not *his* problem, thank goodness. He was merely the Captain, not the Cruise Director.

The human workers waved to him, and the 'simps' flashed toothy smiles, as he walked through the confusion, into the already completed Skylounge. This was his favourite place in the whole ship, and he knew that once she was operating he would never again have it all to himself. He would allow himself just five minutes of private enjoyment.

He called the bridge, checked that everything was still in order, and relaxed into one of the comfortable swivel chairs. Below, in a curve that delighted the eye, was the unbroken silver sweep of the ship's envelope. He was perched at the highest point, surveying the whole immensity of the largest vehicle ever built. And when he had tired of that – all the way out to the horizon was the fantastic wilderness carved by the Colorado River in half a billion years of time.

Apart from the camera platform (it had now fallen back and was filming from amidships) he had the sky to himself. It was blue and empty, clear down to the horizon. In his grandfather's day, Falcon knew, it would have been streaked with vapour trails and stained with smoke. Both had gone: the aerial garbage had vanished with the primitive technologies that spawned it, and the long-distance transportation of this age arced too far beyond the stratosphere for any sight or sound of it to reach Earth. Once again, the lower atmosphere belonged to the birds and the clouds – and now to *Queen Elizabeth IV*.

It was true, as the old pioneers had said at the beginning of the twentieth century: this was the only way to travel – in silence and luxury, breathing the air around you and not cut off from it, near enough to the surface to watch the ever-changing beauty of land and sea. The subsonic jets of the 1980s, packed with hundreds of passengers seated ten abreast, could not even begin to match such comfort and spaciousness.

Of course, the *Queen* would never be an economic proposition, and even if her projected sister ships were built, only a few of the world's quarter of a billion inhabitants would ever enjoy this silent gliding through the sky. But a secure and prosperous global society could afford such follies and indeed needed them for their novelty and entertainment. There were at least a million men on Earth whose discretionary income exceeded a thousand new dollars a year, so the *Queen* would not lack for passengers.

Falcon's pocket communicator beeped. The co-pilot was calling from the bridge.

'OK for rendezvous, Captain? We've got all the data we need from this run, and the TV people are getting impatient.'

Falcon glanced at the camera platform, now matching his speed a tenth of a mile away.

'OK,' he replied. 'Proceed as arranged. I'll watch from here.'

He walked back through the busy chaos of the Observation Deck so that he could have a better view amidships. As he did so, he could feel the change of vibration underfoot; by the time he had reached the rear of the lounge, the ship had come to rest. Using his master key, he let himself out on to the small external platform flaring from the end of the deck; half a dozen people could stand here, with only low guardrails separating them from the vast sweep of the envelope – and from the ground, thousands of feet below. It was an exciting place to be, and perfectly safe even when the ship was travelling at speed, for it was in the dead air behind the huge dorsal blister of the Observation Deck. Nevertheless, it was not intended that the passengers would have access to it; the view was a little too vertiginous.

The covers of the forward cargo hatch had already opened like giant trap doors, and the camera platform was hovering above them, preparing to descend. Along this route, in the years to come, would travel thousands of passengers and tons of supplies. Only on rare occasions would the *Queen* drop down to sea level and dock with her floating base.

A sudden gust of cross wind slapped Falcon's cheek, and he tightened his grip on the guardrail. The Grand Canyon was a bad place for turbulence, though he did not expect much at this altitude. Without any real anxiety, he focused his attention on the descending platform, now about a hundred and fifty feet above the ship. He knew that the highly skilled operator who was flying the remotely controlled vehicle had performed this simple manoeuvre a dozen times already; it was inconceivable that he would have any difficulties.

Yet he seemed to be reacting rather sluggishly. That last gust had drifted the platform almost to the edge of the open hatchway. Surely the pilot could have corrected before this . . . Did he have a control problem? It was very unlikely; these remotes had multiple-redundancy, fail-safe takeovers, and any number of backup systems. Accidents were almost unheard of.

But there he went again, off to the left. Could the pilot be *drunk*? Improbable though that seemed, Falcon considered it seriously for a moment. Then he reached for his microphone switch.

Once again, without warning, he was slapped violently in the face. He hardly felt it, for he was staring in horror at the camera platform. The distant operator was fighting for control, trying to balance the craft on its jets – but he was only making matters worse. The oscillations increased – twenty degrees, forty, sixty, ninety . . .

'Switch to automatic, you fool!' Falcon shouted uselessly into his microphone. 'Your manual control's not working!'

The platform flipped over on its back. The jets no longer supported it, but drove it swiftly downward. They had suddenly become allies of the gravity they had fought until this moment.

Falcon never heard the crash, though he felt it; he was

already inside the Observation Deck, racing for the elevator that would take him down to the bridge. Workmen shouted at him anxiously, asking what had happened. It would be many months before he knew the answer to that question.

Just as he was stepping into the elevator cage, he changed his mind. What if there was a power failure? Better be on the safe side, even if it took longer and time was the essence. He began to run down the spiral stairway enclosing the shaft.

Halfway down he paused for a second to inspect the damage. That damned platform had gone clear through the ship, rupturing two of the gas cells as it did so. They were still collapsing slowly, in great falling veils of plastic. He was not worried about the loss of lift – the ballast could easily take care of that, as long as eight cells remained intact. Far more serious was the possibility of structural damage. Already he could hear the great latticework around him groaning and protesting under its abnormal loads. It was not enough to have sufficient lift; unless it was properly distributed, the ship would break her back.

He was just resuming his descent when a superchimp, shrieking with fright, came racing down the elevator shaft, moving with incredible speed, hand over hand, along the *outside* of the latticework. In its terror, the poor beast had torn off its company uniform, perhaps in an unconscious attempt to regain the freedom of its ancestors.

Falcon, still descending as swiftly as he could, watched its approach with some alarm. A distraught simp was a powerful and potentially dangerous animal, especially if fear overcame its conditioning. As it overtook him, it started to call out a string of words, but they were all jumbled together, and the only one he could recognize was a plaintive, frequently repeated 'boss'. Even now, Falcon realized, it looked towards humans for guidance. He felt sorry for the creature, involved in a man-made disaster beyond its comprehension, and for which it bore no responsibility.

It stopped opposite him, on the other side of the lattice; there was nothing to prevent it from coming through the open framework if it wished. Now its face was only inches from his, and he was looking straight into the terrified eyes. Never before had he been so close to a simp, and able to study its features in such detail. He felt that strange mingling of kinship and discomfort that all men experience when they gaze thus into the mirror of time.

His presence seemed to have calmed the creature. Falcon pointed up the shaft, back towards the Observation Deck, and said very clearly and precisely: 'Boss – boss – *go*.' To his relief, the simp understood; it gave him a grimace that might have been a smile, and at once started to race back the way it had come. Falcon had given it the best advice he could. If any safety remained aboard the *Queen*, it was in that direction. But his duty lay in the other.

He had almost completed his descent when, with a sound of rending metal, the vessel pitched nose down, and the lights went out. But he could still see quite well, for a shaft of sunlight streamed through the open hatch and the huge tear in the envelope. Many years ago he had stood in a great cathedral nave watching the light pouring through the stained-glass windows and forming pools of multicoloured radiance on the ancient flagstones. The dazzling shaft of sunlight through the ruined fabric high above reminded him of that moment. He was in a cathedral of metal, falling down the sky.

When he reached the bridge, and was able for the first time to look outside, he was horrified to see how close the ship was to the ground. Only three thousand feet below were the beautiful and deadly pinnacles of rock and the red rivers of mud that were still carving their way down into the past. There was no level area anywhere in sight where a ship as large as the *Queen* could come to rest on an even keel.

A glance at the display board told him that all the ballast had gone. However, rate of descent had been reduced to a few yards a second; they still had a fighting chance.

Without a word, Falcon eased himself into the pilot's seat and took over such control as still remained. The instrument board showed him everything he wished to know; speech was superfluous. In the background, he could hear the Communications Officer giving a running report over the radio. By this time, all the news channels of Earth would have been preempted, and he could imagine the utter frustration of the programme controllers. One of the most spectacular wrecks in history was occurring – without a single camera to record it. The last moments of the *Queen* would never fill millions with awe and terror, as had those of the *Hindenburg*, a century and a half before.

Now the ground was only about seventeen hundred feet away, still coming up slowly. Though he had full thrust, he had not dared to use it, lest the weakened structure collapse; but now he realized that he had no choice. The wind was taking them towards a fork in the canyon, where the river was split by a wedge of rock like the prow of some gigantic fossilized ship of stone. If she continued on her present course, the *Queen* would straddle that triangular plateau and come to rest with at least a third of her length jutting out over nothingness; she would snap like a rotten stick.

Far away, above the sound of straining metal and escaping gas, came the familiar whistle of the jets as Falcon opened up the lateral thrusters. The ship staggered, and began to slew to port. The shriek of tearing metal was now almost continuous – and the rate of descent had started to increase ominously. A glance at the damage-control board showed that cell number five had just gone.

The ground was only yards away. Even now, he could not tell whether his manoeuvre would succeed or fail. He switched the thrust vectors over to vertical, giving maximum lift to reduce the force of impact.

The crash seemed to last for ever. It was not violent – merely prolonged, and irresistible. It seemed that the whole universe was falling about them.

The sound of crunching metal came nearer, as if some great beast were eating its way through the dying ship.

Then floor and ceiling closed upon him like a vice.

2. 'BECAUSE IT'S THERE'

'Why do you want to go to Jupiter?'

'As Springer said when he lifted for Pluto – "because it's there".'

'Thanks. Now we've got *that* out of the way – the real reason.'

Howard Falcon smiled, though only those who knew him well could have interpreted the slight, leathery grimace. Webster was one of them; for more than twenty years they had shared triumphs and disasters – including the greatest disaster of all.

'Well, Springer's cliché is still valid. We've landed on all the terrestrial planets, but none of the gas giants. They are the only real challenge left in the solar system.'

'An expensive one. Have you worked out the cost?'

'As well as I can; here are the estimates. Remember, though – this isn't a one-shot mission, but a transportation system. Once it's proved out, it can be used over and over again. And it will open up not merely Jupiter, but *all* the giants.'

Webster looked at the figures, and whistled.

'Why not start with an easier planet – Uranus, for example? Half the gravity, and less than half the escape velocity. Quieter weather, too – if that's the right word for it.'

Webster had certainly done his homework. But that, of course, was why he was head of Long-Range Planning.

'There's very little saving – when you allow for the extra distance and the logistics problems. For Jupiter, we can use the facilities of Ganymede. Beyond Saturn, we'd have to establish a new supply base.'

Logical, thought Webster; but he was sure that it was not the important reason. Jupiter was lord of the solar system; Falcon would be interested in no lesser challenge.

'Besides,' Falcon continued, 'Jupiter is a major scientific scandal. It's more than a hundred years since its radio storms were discovered, but we still don't know what causes them – and the Great Red Spot is as big a mystery as ever. That's why I can get matching funds from the Bureau of Astronautics. Do you know how many probes they have dropped into that atmosphere?'

'A couple of hundred, I believe.'

'*Three* hundred and twenty-six, over the last fifty years – about a quarter of them total failures. Of course, they've learned a hell of a lot, but they've barely scratched the planet. Do you realize how *big* it is?'

'More than ten times the size of Earth.'

'Yes, yes – but do you know what that really means?'

Falcon pointed to the large globe in the corner of Webster's office.

'Look at India – how small it seems. Well, if you skinned Earth and spread it out on the surface of Jupiter, it would look about as big as India does here.'

There was a long silence while Webster contemplated the equation: Jupiter is to Earth as Earth is to India. Falcon had – deliberately, of course – chosen the best possible example . . .

Was it already ten years ago? Yes, it must have been. The crash lay seven years in the past (*that* date was engraved on his heart), and those initial tests had taken place three years before the first and last flight of the *Queen Elizabeth*.

Ten years ago, then, Commander (no, Lieutenant) Falcon had invited him to a preview – a three-day drift across the northern plains of India, within sight of the Himalayas. 'Perfectly safe,' he had promised. 'It will get you away from the office – and will teach you what this whole thing is about.'

Webster had not been disappointed. Next to his first journey to the Moon, it had been the most memorable experience of his life. And yet, as Falcon had assured him, it had been perfectly safe, and quite uneventful.

They had taken off from Srinagar just before dawn, with the huge silver bubble of the balloon already catching the first light of the Sun. The ascent had been made in total silence; there were none of the roaring propane burners that had lifted the hot-air balloons of an earlier age. All the heat they needed came from the little pulsed-fusion reactor, weighing only about two hundred and twenty pounds, hanging in the open mouth of the envelope. While they were climbing, its laser was zapping ten times a second, igniting the merest whiff of deuterium fuel. Once they had reached altitude, it would fire only a few times a minute, making up for the heat lost through the great gasbag overhead.

And so, even while they were almost a mile above the ground, they could hear dogs barking, people shouting, bells ringing. Slowly the vast, Sun-smitten landscape expanded around them. Two hours later, they had levelled out at three miles and were taking frequent draughts of oxygen. They could relax and admire the scenery; the on-board instrumentation was doing all the work – gathering the information that would be required by the designers of the still-unnamed liner of the skies.

It was a perfect day. The southwest monsoon would not break for another month, and there was hardly a cloud in the sky. Time seemed to have come to a stop; they resented the hourly radio reports which interrupted their reverie. And all around, to the horizon and far beyond, was that infinite, ancient landscape, drenched with history – a patchwork of villages, fields, temples, lakes, irrigation canals . . .

With a real effort, Webster broke the hypnotic spell of that ten-year-old memory. It had converted him to lighter-than-air flight – and it had made him realize the enormous size of India, even in a world that could be circled within ninety minutes. And yet, he repeated to himself, Jupiter is to Earth as Earth is to India . . .

'Granted your argument,' he said, 'and supposing the funds are available, there's another question you have to answer. Why should you do better than the – what is it – three hundred and twenty-six robot probes that have already made the trip?'

'I am better qualified than they were – as an observer, and as a pilot. *Especially* as a pilot. Don't forget – I've more experience of lighter-than-air flight than anyone in the world.'

'You could still serve as controller, and sit safely on Ganymede.'

'*But that's just the point!* They've already done that. Don't you remember what killed the *Queen*?'

Webster knew perfectly well; but he merely answered: 'Go on.'

'*Time lag – time lag!* That idiot of a platform controller thought he was using a local radio circuit. But he'd been accidentally switched through a satellite – oh, maybe it wasn't his fault, but he should have noticed. That's a half-second time lag for the round trip. Even then it wouldn't have mattered flying in calm air. It was the turbulence over the Grand Canyon that did it. When the platform tipped, and he corrected for that – it had already tipped the other way. Ever tried to drive a car over a bumpy road with a half-second delay in the steering?'

'No, and I don't intend to try. But I can imagine it.'

'Well, Ganymede is a million kilometers from Jupiter. That means a round-trip delay of six seconds. No, you need a controller on the spot – to handle emergencies in real time. Let me show you something. Mind if I use this?'

'Go ahead.'

Falcon picked up a postcard that was lying on Webster's desk; they were almost obsolete on Earth, but this one showed a 3-D view of a Martian landscape, and was decorated with exotic and expensive stamps. He held it so that it dangled vertically.

'This is an old trick, but helps to make my point. Place your thumb and finger on either side, not quite touching. That's right.'

Webster put out his hand, almost but not quite gripping the card.

'Now catch it.'

Falcon waited for a few seconds; then, without warning, he let go of the card. Webster's thumb and finger closed on empty air.

'I'll do it again, just to show there's no deception. You see?'

Once again, the falling card had slipped through Webster's fingers.

'Now you try it on me.'

This time, Webster grasped the card and dropped it without warning. It had scarcely moved before Falcon had caught it. Webster almost imagined he could hear a click, so swift was the other's reaction.

'When they put me together again,' Falcon remarked in an expressionless voice, 'the surgeons made some improvements. This is one of them – and there are others. I want to make the most of them. Jupiter is the place where I can do it.'

Webster stared for long seconds at the fallen card, absorbing the improbable colours of the Trivium Charontis Escarpment. Then he said quietly: 'I understand. How long do you think it will take?'

'With your help, plus the Bureau, plus all the science foundation we can drag in – oh, three years. Then a year for trials – we'll have to send in at least two test models. So, with luck – five years.'

'That's about what I thought. I hope you get your luck; you've earned it. But there's one thing I won't do.'

'What's that?'

'Next time you go ballooning, don't expect *me* as passenger.'

3. THE WORLD OF THE GODS

The fall from Jupiter V to Jupiter itself takes only three and a half hours. Few men could have slept on so awesome a journey. Sleep was a weakness that Howard Falcon hated, and the little he still required brought dreams that time had not yet been able to exorcize. But he could expect no rest in the three days that lay ahead, and must seize what he could during the long fall down into that ocean of clouds, some sixty thousand miles below.

As soon as *Kon-Tiki* had entered her transfer orbit and all the computer checks were satisfactory, he prepared for the last sleep he might ever know. It seemed appropriate that at almost the same moment Jupiter eclipsed the bright and tiny Sun as he swept into the monstrous shadow of the planet. For a few minutes a strange golden twilight enveloped the ship; then a quarter of the sky became an utterly black hole in space, while the rest was a blaze of stars. No matter how far one travelled across the solar system, *they* never changed; these same constellations now shone on Earth, millions of miles away. The only novelties here were the small, pale crescents of Callisto and Ganymede; doubtless there were a dozen other moons up there in the sky, but they were all much too tiny, and too distant, for the unaided eye to pick them out.

'Closing down for two hours,' he reported to the mother ship, hanging almost a thousand miles above the desolate rocks of Jupiter V, in the radiation shadow of the tiny satellite. If it never served any other useful purpose, Jupiter V was a cosmic bulldozer perpetually sweeping up the charged particles that made it unhealthy to linger close to Jupiter. Its wake was almost free of radiation, and there a ship could park in perfect safety, while death sleeted invisibly all around.

Falcon switched on the sleep inducer, and consciousness faded swiftly out as the electric pulses surged gently through his brain. While *Kon-Tiki* fell towards Jupiter, gaining speed second by second in that enormous gravitational field, he slept without dreams. They always came when he awoke; and he had brought his nightmares with him from Earth.

Yet he never dreamed of the crash itself, though he often found himself again face to face with that terrified super-chimp, as he descended the spiral stairway between the collapsing gasbags. None of the simps had survived; those that were not killed outright were so badly injured that they had been painlessly 'euthed'. He sometimes wondered why he dreamed only of this doomed creature – which he had never met before the last minutes of its life – and not of the friends and colleagues he had lost aboard the dying *Queen*.

The dream he feared most always began with his first return to consciousness. There had been little physical pain; in fact, there had been no sensation of any kind. He was in darkness and silence, and did not even seem to be breathing. And – strangest of all – he could not locate his limbs. He could move neither his hands nor his feet, because he did not know where they were.

The silence had been the first to yield. After hours, or days, he had become aware of a faint throbbing, and eventually, after long thought, he deduced that this was the beating of his own heart. That was the first of his many mistakes.

Then there had been faint pinpricks, sparkles of light, ghosts of pressures upon still-unresponsive limbs. One by one his senses had returned, and pain had come with them. He had had to learn everything anew, recapitulating infancy and babyhood. Though his memory was unaffected, and he could understand words that were spoken to him, it was months before he was able to answer except by the flicker of an eyelid. He could remember the moments of triumph when he had spoken the first word, turned the page of a book – and, finally, learned to move under his own power. *That* was a victory indeed, and it had taken him almost two years to prepare for it. A hundred times he had envied that dead superchimp, but *he* had been given no choice. The doctors had made their decision – and now, twelve years later, he was where no human being had ever travelled before, and moving faster than any man in history.

Kon-Tiki was just emerging from shadow, and the Jovian dawn bridged the sky ahead in a titanic bow of light, when the persistent buzz of the alarm dragged Falcon up from sleep. The inevitable nightmares (he had been trying to summon a nurse, but did not even have the strength to push the button) swiftly faded from consciousness. The greatest – and perhaps last – adventure of his life was before him.

He called Mission Control, now almost sixty thousand miles away and falling swiftly below the curve of Jupiter, to report that everything was in order. His velocity had just passed thirty-one miles a second (*that* was one for the books) and in half an hour *Kon-Tiki* would hit the outer fringes of the atmosphere, as he started on the most difficult re-entry in the entire solar system. Although scores of probes had survived this flaming ordeal, they had been tough, solidly packed masses of instrumentation, able to withstand several hundred gravities of drag. *Kon-Tiki* would hit peaks of thirty g's, and would average more than ten, before she came to rest in the upper reaches of the Jovian atmosphere. Very carefully and thoroughly, Falcon began to attach the elaborate system of restraints that would anchor him to the walls of the cabin. When he had finished, he was virtually a part of the ship's structure.

The clock was counting backwards; one hundred seconds to re-entry. For better or worse, he was committed. In a minute and a half, he would graze the Jovian atmosphere, and would be caught irrevocably in the grip of the giant.

The countdown was three seconds late – not at all bad, considering the unknowns involved. From beyond the walls of the capsule came a ghostly sighing, which rose steadily to a high-pitched, screaming roar. The noise was quite different from that of a re-entry on Earth or Mars; in this thin atmosphere of hydrogen and helium, all sounds were transformed a couple of octaves upward. On Jupiter, even thunder would have falsetto overtones.

With the rising scream came mounting weight; within seconds, he was completely immobilized. His field of vision contracted until it embraced only the clock and the accelerometer; fifteen g, and four hundred and eighty seconds to go . . .

He never lost consciousness; but then, he had not expected to. *Kon-Tiki*'s trail through the Jovian atmosphere must be really spectacular – by this time, thousands of miles long. Five hundred seconds after entry, the drag began to taper off: ten g, five g, two . . . Then weight vanished almost completely. He was falling free, all his enormous orbital velocity destroyed.

There was a sudden jolt as the incandescent remnants of the heat shield were jettisoned. It had done its work and would not be needed again; Jupiter could have it now. He released all but two of the restraining buckles, and waited for the automatic sequencer to start the next, and most critical, series of events.

He did not see the first drogue parachute pop out, but he could feel the slight jerk, and the rate of fall diminished immediately. *Kon-Tiki* had lost all her horizontal speed and was going straight down at almost a thousand miles an hour. Everything depended on what happened in the next sixty seconds.

There went the second drogue. He looked up through the overhead window and saw, to his immense relief, that clouds of glittering foil were billowing out behind the falling ship. Like a great flower unfurling, the thousands of cubic yards of the balloon spread out across the sky, scooping up the thin gas until it was fully inflated. *Kon-Tiki*'s rate of fall dropped to a few miles an hour and remained constant. Now there was plenty of time; it would take him days to fall all the way down to the surface of Jupiter.

But he would get there eventually, even if he did nothing about it. The balloon overhead was merely acting as an efficient parachute. It was providing no lift; nor could it do so, while the gas inside and out was the same.

With its characteristic and rather disconcerting crack the fusion reactor started up, pouring torrents of heat into the envelope overhead. Within five minutes, the rate of fall had become zero; within six, the ship had started to rise. According to the radar altimeter, it had levelled out at about two hundred and sixty-seven miles above the surface – or whatever passed for a surface on Jupiter.

Only one kind of balloon will work in an atmosphere of hydrogen, which is the lightest of all gases – and that is a hot-hydrogen balloon. As long as the fuser kept ticking over, Falcon could remain aloft, drifting across a world that could hold a hundred Pacifics. After travelling over three hundred million miles, *Kon-Tiki* had at last begun to justify her name. She was an aerial raft, adrift upon the currents of the Jovian atmosphere.

Though a whole new world was lying around him, it was more than an hour before Falcon could examine the view. First he had to check all the capsule's systems and test its response to the controls. He had to learn how much extra heat was necessary to produce a desired rate of ascent, and how much gas he must vent in order to descend. Above all, there was the question of stability. He must adjust the length of the cables attaching his capsule to the huge, pear-shaped balloon, to damp out vibrations and get the smoothest possible ride. Thus far, he was lucky; at this level, the wind was steady, and the Doppler reading on the invisible surface gave him a ground speed of two hundred and seventeen and a half miles an hour. For Jupiter, that was modest; winds of up to a thousand had been observed. But mere speed was, of course, unimportant; the real danger was turbulence. If he ran into that, only skill and experience and swift reaction could save him – and these were not matters that could yet be programmed into a computer.

Not until he was satisfied that he had got the feel of his strange craft did Falcon pay any attention to Mission Control's pleadings. Then he deployed the booms carrying the instrumentation and the atmospheric samplers. The capsule now resembled a rather untidy Christmas tree, but still rode smoothly down the Jovian winds while it radioed its torrents of information to the recorders on the ship miles above. And now, at last, he could look around . . .

His first impression was unexpected, and even a little disappointing. As far as the scale of things was concerned, he might have been ballooning over an ordinary cloudscape on Earth. The horizon seemed at a normal distance; there was no feeling at all that he was on a world eleven times the diameter of his own. Then he looked at the infrared radar, sounding the layers of atmosphere beneath him – and knew how badly his eyes had been deceived.

The layer of clouds apparently about three miles away was really more than thirty-seven miles below. And the horizon, whose distance he would have guessed at about one hundred and twenty-five, was actually eighteen hundred miles from the ship.

The crystalline clarity of the hydrohelium atmosphere and the enormous curvature of the planet had fooled him completely. It was even harder to judge distances here than on the Moon; everything he saw must be multiplied by at least ten.

It was a simple matter, and he should have been prepared for it. Yet somehow, it disturbed him profoundly. He did not feel that Jupiter was huge, but that *he* had shrunk – to a tenth of his normal size. Perhaps, with time, he would grow accustomed to the inhuman scale of this world; yet as he stared towards that unbelievably distant horizon, he felt as if a wind colder than the atmosphere around him was blowing through his soul. Despite all his arguments, this might never be a place for man. He could well be both the first and the last to descend through the clouds of Jupiter.

The sky above was almost black, except for a few wisps of ammonia cirrus perhaps twelve miles overhead. It was cold up there, on the fringes of space, but both pressure and temperature increased rapidly with depth. At the level where *Kon-Tiki* was drifting now, it was fifty below zero, and the pressure was five atmospheres. Sixty-five miles farther down, it would be as warm as equatorial Earth, and the pressure about the same as at the bottom of one of the shallower seas. Ideal conditions for life . . .

A quarter of the brief Jovian day had already gone; the Sun was halfway up the sky, but the light on the unbroken cloudscape below had a curious mellow quality. That extra three hundred million miles had robbed the Sun of all its power. Though the sky was clear, Falcon found himself continually thinking that it was a heavily overcast day. When night fell, the onset of darkness would be swift indeed; though it was still morning, there was a sense of autumnal twilight in the air. But autumn, of course, was something that never came to Jupiter. There were no seasons here.

Kon-Tiki had come down in the exact centre of the equatorial zone – the least colourful part of the planet. The sea of clouds that stretched out to the horizon were tinted a pale salmon;

there were none of the yellows and pinks and even reds that banded Jupiter at higher altitudes. The Great Red Spot itself – most spectacular of all of the planet's features – lay thousands of miles to the south. It had been a temptation to descend there, but the south tropical disturbance was unusually active, with currents reaching over nine hundred miles an hour. It would have been asking for trouble to head into that maelstrom of unknown forces. The Great Red Spot and its mysteries would have to wait for future expeditions.

The Sun, moving across the sky twice as swiftly as it did on Earth, was now nearing the zenith and had become eclipsed by the great silver canopy of the balloon. *Kon-Tiki* was still drifting swiftly and smoothly westward at a steady two hundred and seventeen and a half, but only the radar gave any indication of this. Was it always as calm here? Falcon asked himself. The scientists who had talked learnedly of the Jovian doldrums, and had predicted that the equator would be the quietest place, seemed to know what they were talking about, after all. He had been profoundly sceptical of all such forecasts, and had agreed with one unusually modest researcher who had told him bluntly: 'There are *no* experts on Jupiter.' Well, there would be at least one by the end of this day.

If he managed to survive until then.

4. THE VOICES OF THE DEEP

That first day, the Father of the Gods smiled upon him. It was as calm and peaceful here on Jupiter as it had been, years ago, when he was drifting with Webster across the plains of northern India. Falcon had time to master his new skills, until *Kon-Tiki* seemed an extension of his own body. Such luck was more than he had dared to hope for, and he began to wonder what price he might have to pay for it.

The five hours of daylight were almost over; the clouds below were full of shadows, which gave them a massive solidity they had not possessed when the Sun was higher. Colour was swiftly draining from the sky, except in the west itself, where a band of deepening purple lay along the horizon. Above this band was the thin crescent of a closer moon, pale and bleached against the utter blackness beyond.

With a speed perceptible to the eye, the Sun went straight down over the edge of Jupiter, over eighteen hundred miles away. The stars came out in their legions – and there was the beautiful evening star of Earth, on the very frontier of twilight, reminding him how far he was from home. It followed the Sun down into the west. Man's first night on Jupiter had begun.

With the onset of darkness, *Kon-Tiki* started to sink. The balloon was no longer heated by the feeble sunlight and was losing a small part of its buoyancy. Falcon did nothing to increase lift; he had expected this and was planning to descend.

The invisible cloud deck was still over thirty miles below, and he would reach it about midnight. It showed up clearly on the infrared radar, which also reported that it contained a vast array of complex carbon compounds, as well as the usual hydrogen, helium and ammonia. The chemists were dying for samples of that fluffy, pinkish stuff; though some atmospheric probes had already gathered a few grams, that had only whetted their appetites. Half the basic molecules of life were here, floating high above the surface of Jupiter. And where there was food, could life be far away? That was the question that, after more than a hundred years, no one had been able to answer.

The infrared was blocked by the clouds, but the microwave radar sliced right through and showed layer after layer, all the way down to the hidden surface almost two hundred and fifty miles below. That was barred to him by enormous pressures and temperatures; not even robot probes had ever reached it intact. It lay in tantalizing inaccessibility at the bottom of the radar screen, slightly fuzzy, and showing a curious granular structure that his equipment could not resolve.

An hour after sunset, he dropped his first probe. It fell swiftly for about sixty miles, then began to float in the denser atmosphere, sending back torrents of radio signals, which he relayed to Mission Control. Then there was nothing else to do until sunrise, except to keep an eye on the rate of descent, monitor the instruments, and answer occasional queries. While she was drifting in this steady current, *Kon-Tiki* could look after herself.

Just before midnight, a woman controller came on watch and introduced herself with the usual pleasantries. Ten minutes later she called again, her voice at once serious and excited.

'Howard! Listen in on Channel forty-six – high gain.'

Channel forty-six? There were so many telemetering circuits that he knew the numbers of only those that were critical; but as soon as he threw the switch, he recognized this one. He was plugged in to the microphone on the probe, floating more than eighty miles below him in an atmosphere now almost as dense as water.

At first, there was only a soft hiss of whatever strange winds stirred down in the darkness of that unimaginable world. And then, out of the background noise, there slowly emerged a booming vibration that grew louder and louder, like the beating of a gigantic drum. It was so low that it was felt as much as heard, and the beats steadily increased their tempo, though the pitch never changed. Now it was a swift, almost infrasonic throbbing. Then, suddenly, in mid-vibration, it stopped – so abruptly that the mind could not accept the silence, but memory continued to manufacture a ghostly echo in the deepest caverns of the brain.

It was the most extraordinary sound that Falcon had ever heard, even among the multitudinous noises of Earth. He could think of no natural phenomenon that could have caused it; nor was it like the cry of any animal, not even one of the great whales . . .

It came again, following exactly the same pattern. Now that he was prepared for it, he estimated the length of the sequence; from first faint throb to final crescendo, it lasted just over ten seconds.

And this time there was a real echo, very faint and far away.

Perhaps it came from one of the many reflecting layers, deeper in this stratified atmosphere; perhaps it was another, more distant source. Falcon waited for a second echo, but it never came.

Mission Control reacted quickly and asked him to drop another probe at once. With two microphones operating, it would be possible to find the approximate location of the sources. Oddly enough, none of *Kon-Tiki*'s own external mikes could detect anything except wind noises. The boomings, whatever they were, must have been trapped and channelled beneath an atmospheric reflecting layer far below.

They were coming, it was soon discovered, from a cluster of sources about twelve hundred miles away. The distance gave no indication of their power; in Earth's oceans, quite feeble sounds could travel equally far. And as for the obvious assumption that living creatures were responsible, the Chief Exobiologist quickly ruled that out.

'I'll be very disappointed,' said Dr Brenner, 'if there are no micro-organisms or plants here. But nothing like animals, because there's no free oxygen. All biochemical reactions on Jupiter must be low-energy ones – there's just no way an active creature could generate enough power to function.'

Falcon wondered if this was true; he had heard the argument before, and reserved judgement.

'In any case,' continued Brenner, 'some of those sound waves are a hundred yards long! Even an animal as big as a whale couldn't produce them. They *must* have a natural origin.'

Yes, that seemed plausible, and probably the physicists would be able to come up with an explanation. What would a blind alien make, Falcon wondered, of the sounds he might hear when standing beside a stormy sea, or a geyser, or a volcano, or a waterfall? He might well attribute them to some huge beast.

About an hour before sunrise the voices of the deep died away, and Falcon began to busy himself with preparation for the dawn of his second day. *Kon-Tiki* was now only three miles above the nearest cloud layer; the external pressure had risen to ten atmospheres, and the temperature was a tropical thirty degrees. A man could be comfortable here with no more equipment than a breathing mask and the right grade of heliox mixture.

'We've some good news for you,' Mission Control reported, soon after dawn. 'The cloud layer's breaking up. You'll have partial clearing in an hour – but watch out for turbulence.'

'I've already noticed some,' Falcon answered. 'How far down will I be able to see?'

'At least twelve miles, down to the second thermocline. *That* cloud deck is solid – it never breaks.'

And it's out of my reach, Falcon told himself; the temperature down there must be over a hundred degrees. This was the first time that any balloonist had ever had to worry, not about his ceiling, but about his basement!

Ten minutes later he could see what Mission Control had already observed from its superior vantage point. There was a change in colour near the horizon, and the cloud layer had become ragged and humpy, as if something had torn it open. He turned up his little nuclear furnace and gave *Kon-Tiki* another three miles of altitude, so that he could get a better view.

The sky below was clearing rapidly, completely, as if something was dissolving the solid overcast. An abyss was opening before his eyes. A moment later he sailed out over the edge of a cloud canyon about twelve miles deep and six hundred miles wide.

A new world lay spread beneath him; Jupiter had stripped away one of its many veils. The second layer of clouds, unattainably far below, was much darker in colour than the first. It was almost salmon pink, and curiously mottled with little islands of brick red. They were all oval-shaped, with their long axes pointing east-west, in the direction of the prevailing wind. There were hundreds of them, all about the same size, and they reminded Falcon of puffy little cumulus clouds in the terrestrial sky.

He reduced buoyancy, and *Kon-Tiki* began to drop down the face of the dissolving cliff. It was then that he noticed the snow.

White flakes were forming in the air and drifting slowly downward. Yet it was much too warm for snow – and, in any event, there was scarcely a trace of water at this altitude. Moreover, there was no glitter or sparkle about these flakes as they went cascading down into the depths. When, presently, a few landed on an instrument boom outside the main viewing port, he saw that they were a dull, opaque white – not crystalline at all – and quite large – several inches across. They looked like wax, and Falcon guessed that this was precisely what they were. Some chemical reaction was taking place in the atmosphere around him, condensing out the hydrocarbons floating in the Jovian air.

About sixty miles ahead, a disturbance was taking place in the cloud layer. The little red ovals were being jostled around, and were beginning to form a spiral – the familiar cyclonic pattern so common in the meteorology of Earth. The vortex was emerging with astonishing speed; if that was a storm ahead, Falcon told himself, he was in big trouble.

And then his concern changed to wonder – and to fear. What was developing in his line of flight was not a storm at all. Something enormous – something scores of miles across – was rising through the clouds.

The reassuring thought that it, too, might be a cloud – a thunderhead boiling up from the lower levels of the atmosphere – lasted only a few seconds. No; this was *solid*. It shouldered its way through the pink-and-salmon overcast like an iceberg rising from the deeps.

An *iceberg* floating on hydrogen? That was impossible, of course; but perhaps it was not too remote an analogy. As soon as he focused the telescope upon the enigma, Falcon saw that it was a whitish, crystalline mass, threaded with streaks of red and brown. It must be, he decided, the same stuff as the 'snowflakes' falling around him – a mountain range of wax. And it was not, he soon realized, as solid as he had thought;

around the edges it was continually crumbling and re-forming . . .

'I know what it is,' he radioed Mission Control, which for the last few minutes had been asking anxious questions. 'It's a mass of bubbles – some kind of foam. Hydrocarbon froth. Get the chemists working on . . . *Just a minute!*'

'What is it?' called Mission Control. 'What is it?'

He ignored the frantic pleas from space and concentrated all his mind upon the image in the telescope field. He had to be sure; if he made a mistake, he would be the laughing-stock of the solar system.

Then he relaxed, glanced at the clock, and switched off the nagging voice from Jupiter V.

'Hello, Mission Control,' he said, very formally. 'This is Howard Falcon aboard *Kon-Tiki*. Ephemeris Time nineteen hours twenty-one minutes fifteen seconds. Latitude zero degrees five minutes North. Longitude one hundred five degrees forty-two minutes, System One.

'Tell Dr Brenner that there is life on Jupiter. And it's *big* . . .'

5. THE WHEELS OF POSEIDON

'I'm very happy to be proved wrong,' Dr Brenner radioed back cheerfully. 'Nature always has something up her sleeve. Keep the long-focus camera on target and give us the steadiest pictures you can.'

The things moving up and down those waxen slopes were still too far away for Falcon to make out many details, and they must have been very large to be visible at all at such a distance. Almost black, and shaped like arrowheads, they manoeuvred by slow undulations of their entire bodies, so that they looked rather like giant manta rays, swimming above some tropical reef.

Perhaps they were sky-borne cattle, browsing on the cloud pastures of Jupiter, for they seemed to be feeding along the dark, red-brown streaks that ran like dried-up river beds down the flanks of the floating cliffs. Occasionally, one of them would dive headlong into the mountain of foam and disappear completely from sight.

Kon-Tiki was moving only slowly with respect to the cloud layer below; it would be at least three hours before she was above those ephemeral hills. She was in a race with the Sun. Falcon hoped that darkness would not fall before he could get a good view of the mantas, as he had christened them, as well as the fragile landscape over which they flapped their way.

It was a long three hours. During the whole time, he kept the external microphones on full gain, wondering if here was the source of that booming in the night. The mantas were certainly large enough to have produced it; when he could get an accurate measurement, he discovered that they were almost a hundred yards across the wings. That was three times the length of the largest whale – though he doubted if they could weigh more than a few tons.

Half an hour before sunset, *Kon-Tiki* was almost above the 'mountains'.

'No,' said Falcon, answering Mission Control's repeated questions about the mantas, 'they're still showing no reaction to me. I don't think they're intelligent – they look like harmless vegetarians. And even if they try to chase me, I'm sure they can't reach my altitude.'

Yet he was a little disappointed when the mantas showed not the slightest interest in him as he sailed high above their feeding ground. Perhaps they had no way of detecting his presence. When he examined and photographed them through the telescope, he could see no signs of any sense organs. The creatures were simply huge black deltas, rippling over hills and valleys that, in reality, were little more substantial than the clouds of Earth. Though they looked solid, Falcon knew that anyone who stepped on those white mountains would go crashing through them as if they were made of tissue paper.

At close quarters he could see the myriads of cellules or

bubbles from which they were formed. Some of these were quite large – a yard or so in diameter – and Falcon wondered in what witches' cauldron of hydrocarbons they had been brewed. There must be enough petrochemicals deep down in the atmosphere of Jupiter to supply all Earth's needs for a million years.

The short day had almost gone when he passed over the crest of the waxen hills, and the light was fading rapidly along their lower slopes. There were no mantas on this western side, and for some reason the topography was very different. The foam was sculptured into long, level terraces, like the interior of a lunar crater. He could almost imagine that they were gigantic steps leading down to the hidden surface of the planet.

And on the lowest of those steps, just clear of the swirling clouds that the mountain had displaced when it came surging skyward, was a roughly oval mass, one or two miles across. It was difficult to see, since it was only a little darker than the grey-white foam on which it rested. Falcon's first thought was that he was looking at a forest of pallid trees, like giant mushrooms that had never seen the Sun.

Yes, it must be a forest – he could see hundreds of thin trunks, springing from the white waxy froth in which they were rooted. But the trees were packed astonishingly close together; there was scarcely any space between them. Perhaps it was not a forest, after all, but a single enormous tree – like one of the giant multi-trunked banyans of the East. Once he had seen a banyan tree in Java that was over six hundred and fifty yards across; this monster was at least ten times that size.

The light had almost gone. The cloudscape had turned purple with refracted sunlight, and in a few seconds that, too, would have vanished. In the last light of his second day on Jupiter, Howard Falcon saw – or thought he saw – something that cast the gravest doubts on his interpretation of the white oval.

Unless the dim light had totally deceived him, those hundreds of thin trunks were beating back and forth, in perfect synchronism, like fronds of kelp rocking in the surge.

And the tree was no longer in the place where he had first seen it.

'Sorry about this,' said Mission Control, soon after sunset, 'but we think Source Beta is going to blow within the next hour. Probability seventy per cent.'

Falcon glanced quickly at the chart. Beta – Jupiter latitude one hundred and forty degrees – was over eighteen thousand six hundred miles away and well below his horizon. Even though major eruptions ran as high as ten megatons, he was much too far away for the shock wave to be a serious danger. The radio storm that it would trigger was, however, quite a different matter.

The decameter outbursts that sometimes made Jupiter the most powerful radio source in the whole sky had been discovered back in the 1950s, to the utter astonishment of the astronomers. Now, more than a century later, their real cause was still a mystery. Only the symptoms were understood; the explanation was completely unknown.

The 'volcano' theory had best stood the test of time, although no one imagined that this word had the same meaning on Jupiter as on Earth. At frequent intervals – often several times a day – titanic eruptions occurred in the lower depths of the atmosphere, probably on the hidden surface of the planet itself. A great column of gas, more than six hundred miles high, would start boiling upward as if determined to escape into space.

Against the most powerful gravitational field of all the planets, it had no chance. Yet some traces – a mere few million tons – usually managed to reach the Jovian ionosphere: and when they did, all hell broke loose.

The radiation belts surrounding Jupiter completely dwarf the feeble Van Allen belts of Earth. When they are short-circuited by an ascending column of gas, the result is an electrical discharge millions of times more powerful than any terrestrial flash of lightning; it sends a colossal thunderclap of radio noise flooding across the entire solar system and on out to the stars.

It had been discovered that these radio outbursts came from four main areas of the planet. Perhaps there were weaknesses there that allowed the fires of the interior to break out from time to time. The scientists on Ganymede, largest of Jupiter's many moons, now thought that they could predict the onset of a decameter storm; their accuracy was about as good as a weather forecaster's of the early 1900s.

Falcon did not know whether to welcome or to fear a radio storm; it would certainly add to the value of the mission – if he survived it. His course had been planned to keep as far as possible from the main centres of disturbance, especially the most active one, Source Alpha. As luck would have it, the threatening Beta was the closest to him. He hoped that the distance, almost three-fourths the circumference of Earth, was safe enough.

'Probability ninety per cent,' said Mission Control with a distinct note of urgency. 'And forget that hour. Ganymede says it may be any moment.'

The radio had scarcely fallen silent when the reading on the magnetic field-strength meter started to shoot upward. Before it could go off scale, it reversed and began to drop as rapidly as it had risen. Far away and thousands of miles below, something had given the planet's molten core a titanic jolt.

'There she blows!' called Mission Control.

'Thanks, I already know. When will the storm hit me?'

'You can expect onset in five minutes. Peak in ten.'

Far around the curve of Jupiter, a funnel of gas as wide as the Pacific Ocean was climbing spaceward at thousands of miles an hour. Already, the thunderstorms of the lower atmosphere would be raging around it – but they were nothing compared with the fury that would explode when the radiation belt was reached and began dumping its surplus electrons on to the planet. Falcon began to retract all the instrument booms that were extended out from the capsule. There were no other precautions he could take. It would be four hours before the atmospheric shock wave reached him – but the radio blast, travelling at the speed of light, would be here in a tenth of a second, once the discharge had been triggered.

The radio monitor, scanning back and forth across the spectrum, still showed nothing unusual, just the normal mush of background static. Then Falcon noticed that the noise level was slowly creeping upward. The explosion was gathering its strength.

At such a distance he had never expected to *see* anything. But suddenly a flicker as of far-off heat lightning danced along the eastern horizon. Simultaneously, half the circuit breakers jumped out of the main switchboard, the lights failed, and all communications channels went dead.

He tried to move, but was completely unable to do so. The paralysis that gripped him was not merely psychological; he seemed to have lost all control of his limbs and could feel a painful tingling sensation over his entire body. It was impossible that the electric field could have penetrated this shielded cabin. Yet there was a flickering glow over the instrument board, and he could hear the unmistakable crackle of a brush discharge.

With a series of sharp bangs, the emergency systems went into operation, and the overloads reset themselves. The lights flickered on again. And Falcon's paralysis disappeared as swiftly as it had come.

After glancing at the board to make sure that all circuits were back to normal, he moved quickly to the viewing ports.

There was no need to switch on the inspection lamps – the cables supporting the capsule seemed to be on fire. Lines of light glowing an electric blue against the darkness stretched upward from the main lift ring to the equator of the giant balloon; and rolling slowly along several of them were dazzling balls of fire.

The sight was so strange and so beautiful that it was hard to read any menace in it. Few people, Falcon knew, had ever seen ball lightning from such close quarters – and certainly none had survived if they were riding a hydrogen-filled balloon back in the atmosphere of Earth. He remembered the flaming death of the *Hindenburg*, destroyed by a stray spark when she docked at Lakehurst in 1937; as it had done so often in the past, the horrifying old newsreel film flashed through his mind. But at least that could not happen here, though there was more hydrogen above his head than had ever filled the last of the Zeppelins. It would be a few billion years yet before anyone could light a fire in the atmosphere of Jupiter.

With a sound like briskly frying bacon, the speech circuit came back to life.

'Hello, *Kon-Tiki* – are you receiving? Are you receiving?'

The words were chopped and badly distorted, but intelligible. Falcon's spirits lifted; he had resumed contact with the world of men.

'I receive you,' he said. 'Quite an electrical display, but no damage – so far.'

'Thanks – thought we'd lost you. Please check telemetry channels three, seven, twenty-six. Also gain on camera two. And we don't quite believe the readings on the external ionization probes . . .'

Reluctantly Falcon tore his gaze away from the fascinating pyrotechnic display around *Kon-Tiki*, though from time to time he kept glancing out of the windows. The ball lightning disappeared first, the fiery globes slowly expanding until they reached a critical size, at which they vanished in a gentle explosion. But even an hour later, there were still faint glows around all the exposed metal on the outside of the capsule; and the radio circuits remained noisy until well after midnight.

The remaining hours of darkness were completely uneventful – until just before dawn. Because it came from the east, Falcon assumed that he was seeing the first faint hint of sunrise. Then he realized that it was twenty minutes too early for this – and the glow that had appeared along the horizon was moving towards him even as he watched. It swiftly detached itself from the arch of stars that marked the invisible edge of the planet, and he saw that it was a relatively narrow band, quite sharply defined. The beam of an enormous searchlight appeared to be swinging beneath the clouds.

Perhaps sixty miles behind the first racing bar of light came another, parallel to it and moving at the same speed. And beyond that another, and another – until all the sky flickered with alternating sheets of light and darkness.

By this time, Falcon thought, he had been inured to wonders, and it seemed impossible that this display of pure, soundless luminosity could present the slightest danger. But it was so astonishing, and so inexplicable, that he felt cold, naked fear gnawing at his self-control. No man could look upon such a sight without feeling like a helpless pygmy in the presence of forces beyond his comprehension. Was it possible that, after all, Jupiter carried not only life but also intelligence? And, perhaps, an intelligence that only now was beginning to react to his alien presence?

'Yes, we see it,' said Mission Control, in a voice that echoed his own awe. 'We've no idea what it is. Stand by, we're calling Ganymede.'

The display was slowly fading; the bands racing in from the far horizon were much fainter, as if the energies that powered them were becoming exhausted. In five minutes it was all over; the last faint pulse of light flickered along the western sky and then was gone. Its passing left Falcon with an overwhelming sense of relief. The sight was so hypnotic, and so disturbing, that it was not good for any man's peace of mind to contemplate it too long.

He was more shaken than he cared to admit. The electrical storm was something that he could understand; but *this* was totally incomprehensible.

Mission Control was still silent. He knew that the information banks up on Ganymede were now being searched as men and computers turned their minds to the problem. If no answer could be found there, it would be necessary to call Earth; that would mean a delay of almost an hour. The possibility that even Earth might be unable to help was one that Falcon did not care to contemplate.

He had never before been so glad to hear the voice of Mission Control as when Dr Brenner finally came on the circuit. The biologist sounded relieved, yet subdued – like a man who has just come through some great intellectual crisis.

'Hello, *Kon-Tiki*. We've solved your problem, but we can still hardly believe it.

'What you've been seeing is bioluminescence, very similar to that produced by micro-organisms in the tropical seas of Earth. Here they're in the atmosphere, not the ocean, but the principle is the same.'

'But the pattern,' protested Falcon, 'was so regular – so *artificial*. And it was hundreds of miles across!'

'It was even larger than you imagine; you observed only a small part of it. The whole pattern was over three thousand miles wide and looked like a revolving wheel. You merely saw the spokes, sweeping past you at about six-tenths of a mile a second . . .'

'A *second*!' Falcon could not help interjecting. 'No animals could move that fast!'

'Of course not. Let me explain. What you saw was triggered by the shock wave from Source Beta, moving at the speed of sound.'

'But what about the pattern?' Falcon insisted.

'That's the surprising part. It's a very rare phenomenon, but identical wheels of light – except that they're a thousand times smaller – have been observed in the Persian Gulf and the Indian Ocean. Listen to this: British India Company's *Patna*, Persian Gulf, May 1880, 11:30 P.M. – "an enormous luminous wheel, whirling round, the spokes of which appeared to brush the ship along. The spokes were 200 or 300 yards long . . . each wheel contained about sixteen spokes . . ." And here's one from the Gulf of Omar, dated May 23, 1906: "The intensely bright luminescence approached us rapidly, shooting sharply defined light rays to the west in rapid succession, like the beam from the searchlight of a warship . . . To the left of us, a gigantic fiery wheel formed itself, with spokes that reached as far as one could see. The whole wheel whirled around for two or three minutes . . ." The archive computer on Ganymede dug up about five hundred cases. It would have printed out the lot if we hadn't stopped it in time.'

'I'm convinced – but still baffled.'

'I don't blame you. The full explanation wasn't worked out until late in the twentieth century. It seems that these luminous wheels are the results of submarine earthquakes, and always occur in shallow waters where the shock waves can be reflected and cause standing wave patterns. Sometimes bars, sometimes rotating wheels – the "Wheels of Poseidon", they've been called. The theory was finally proved by making underwater explosions and photographing the results from a satellite. No wonder the sailors used to be superstitious. Who would have believed a thing like *this*?'

So that was it, Falcon told himself. When Source Beta blew its top, it must have sent shock waves in all directions – through the compressed gas of the lower atmosphere, through the solid body of Jupiter itself. Meeting and crisscrossing, those waves must have cancelled here, reinforced there; the whole planet must have rung like a bell.

Yet the explanation did not destroy the sense of wonder and awe; he would never be able to forget those flickering bands of light, racing through the unattainable depths of the Jovian atmosphere. He felt that he was not merely on a strange planet, but in some magical realm between myth and reality.

This was a world where absolutely *anything* could happen, and no man could possibly guess what the future would bring.

And he still had a whole day to go.

6. MEDUSA

When the true dawn finally arrived, it brought a sudden change of weather. *Kon-Tiki* was moving through a blizzard; waxen snowflakes were falling so thickly that visibility was reduced to zero. Falcon began to worry about the weight that might be accumulating on the envelope. Then he noticed that any flakes settling outside the windows quickly disappeared;

Kon-Tiki's continual outpouring of heat was evaporating them as swiftly as they arrived.

If he had been ballooning on Earth, he would also have worried about the possibility of collision. At least that was no danger here; any Jovian mountains were several hundred miles below him. And as for the floating islands of foam, hitting them would probably be like ploughing into slightly hardened soap bubbles.

Nevertheless, he switched on the horizontal radar, which until now had been completely useless; only the vertical beam, giving his distance from the invisible surface, had thus far been of any value. Then he had another surprise.

Scattered across a huge sector of the sky ahead were dozens of large and brilliant echoes. They were completely isolated from one another and apparently hung unsupported in space. Falcon remembered a phrase the earliest aviators had used to describe one of the hazards of their profession: 'clouds stuffed with rocks'. That was a perfect description of what seemed to lie in the track of *Kon-Tiki.*

It was a disconcerting sight; then Falcon again reminded himself that nothing *really* solid could possibly hover in this atmosphere. Perhaps it was some strange meteorological phenomenon. In any case, the nearest echo was about a hundred and twenty-five miles.

He reported to Mission Control, which could provide no explanation. But it gave the welcome news that he would be clear of the blizzard in another thirty minutes.

It did not warn him, however, of the violent cross wind that abruptly grabbed *Kon-Tiki* and swept it almost at right angles to its previous track. Falcon needed all his skill and the maximum use of what little control he had over his ungainly vehicle to prevent it from being capsized. Within minutes he was racing northward at over three hundred miles an hour. Then, as suddenly as it had started, the turbulence ceased; he was still moving at high speed, but in smooth air. He wondered if he had been caught in the Jovian equivalent of a jet stream.

The snow storm dissolved; and he saw what Jupiter had

been preparing for him.

Kon-Tiki had entered the funnel of a gigantic whirlpool, some six hundred miles across. The balloon was being swept along a curving wall of cloud. Overhead, the Sun was shining in a clear sky; but far beneath, this great hole in the atmosphere drilled down to unknown depths until it reached a misty floor where lightning flickered almost continuously.

Though the vessel was being dragged downward so slowly that it was in no immediate danger, Falcon increased the flow of heat into the envelope until *Kon-Tiki* hovered at a constant altitude. Not until then did he abandon the fantastic spectacle outside and consider again the problem of the radar.

The nearest echo was now only about twenty-five miles away. All of them, he quickly realized, were distributed along the wall of the vortex, and were moving with it, apparently caught in the whirlpool like *Kon-Tiki* itself. He aimed the telescope along the radar bearing and found himself looking at a curious mottled cloud that almost filled the field of view.

It was not easy to see, being only a little darker than the whirling wall of mist that formed its background. Not until he had been staring for several minutes did Falcon realize that he had met it once before.

The first time it had been crawling across the drifting mountains of foam, and he had mistaken it for a giant, many-trunked tree. Now at last he could appreciate its real size and complexity and could give it a better name to fix its image in his mind. It did not resemble a tree at all, but a jellyfish – a medusa, such as might be met trailing its tentacles as it drifted along the warm eddies of the Gulf Stream.

This medusa was more than a mile across and its scores of dangling tentacles were hundreds of feet long. They swayed slowly back and forth in perfect unison, taking more than a minute for each complete undulation – almost as if the creature was clumsily rowing itself through the sky.

The other echoes were more distant medusae. Falcon focused the telescope on half a dozen and could see no variations in shape or size. They all seemed to be of the same species, and he wondered just why they were drifting lazily around in this six-hundred-mile orbit. Perhaps they were feeding upon the aerial plankton sucked in by the whirlpool, as *Kon-Tiki* itself had been.

'Do you realize, Howard,' said Dr Brenner, when he had recovered from his initial astonishment, 'that this thing is about a hundred thousand times as large as the biggest whale? And even if it's only a gasbag, it must still weigh a million tons! I can't even guess at its metabolism. It must generate megawatts of heat to maintain its buoyancy.'

'But if it's just a gasbag, why is it such a damn good radar reflector?'

'I haven't the faintest idea. Can you get any closer?'

Brenner's question was not an idle one. If he changed altitude to take advantage of the differing wind velocities, Falcon could approach the medusa as closely as he wished. At the moment, however, he preferred his present twenty-five miles and said so, firmly.

'I see what you mean,' Brenner answered, a little reluctantly. 'Let's stay where we are for the present.' That 'we' gave Falcon a certain wry amusement; an extra sixty thousand miles made a considerable difference in one's point of view.

For the next two hours *Kon-Tiki* drifted uneventfully in the gyre of the great whirlpool, while Falcon experimented with filters and camera contrast, trying to get a clear view of the medusa. He began to wonder if its elusive colouration was some kind of camouflage; perhaps, like many animals of Earth, it was trying to lose itself against its background. That was a trick used by both hunters and hunted.

In which category was the medusa? That was a question he could hardly expect to have answered in the short time that was left to him. Yet just before noon, without the slightest warning, the answer came . . .

Like a squadron of antique jet fighters, five mantas came sweeping through the wall of mist that formed the funnel of the vortex. They were flying in a V formation directly towards the pallid grey cloud of the medusa; and there was no doubt, in Falcon's mind, that they were on the attack. He had been quite wrong to assume that they were harmless vegetarians.

Yet everything happened at such a leisurely pace that it was like watching a slow-motion film. The mantas undulated along at perhaps thirty miles an hour; it seemed ages before they reached the medusa, which continued to paddle imperturbably along at an even slower speed. Huge though they were, the mantas looked tiny beside the monster they were approaching. When they flapped down on its back, they appeared about as large as birds landing on a whale.

Could the medusa defend itself? Falcon wondered. He did not see how the attacking mantas could be in danger as long as they avoided those huge clumsy tentacles. And perhaps their host was not even aware of them; they could be insignificant parasites, tolerated as are fleas upon a dog.

But now it was obvious that the medusa was in distress. With agonizing slowness, it began to tip over like a capsizing ship. After ten minutes it had tilted forty-five degrees; it was also rapidly losing altitude. It was impossible not to feel a sense of pity for the beleaguered monster, and to Falcon the sight brought bitter memories. In a grotesque way, the fall of the medusa was almost a parody of the dying *Queen*'s last moments.

Yet he knew that his sympathies were on the wrong side. High intelligence could develop only among predators – not among the drifting browsers of either sea or air. The mantas were far closer to him than was this monstrous bag of gas. And anyway, who could *really* sympathize with a creature a hundred thousand times larger than a whale?

Then he noticed that the medusa's tactics seemed to be having some effect. The mantas had been disturbed by its slow roll and were flapping heavily away from its back – like gorged vultures interrupted at mealtime. But they did not move very far, continuing to hover a few yards from the still-capsizing monster.

There was a sudden, blinding flash of light synchronized

with a crash of static over the radio. One of the mantas, slowly twisting end over end, was plummeting straight downward. As it fell, a plume of black smoke trailed behind it. The resemblance to an aircraft going down in flames was quite uncanny.

In unison, the remaining mantas dived steeply away from the medusa, gaining speed by losing altitude. They had, within minutes, vanished back into the wall of cloud from which they had emerged. And the medusa, no longer falling, began to roll back towards the horizontal. Soon it was sailing along once more on an even keel, as if nothing had happened.

'Beautiful!' said Dr Brenner, after a moment of stunned silence. 'It's developed electric defences, like some of our eels and rays. But that must have been about a million volts! Can you see any organs that might produce the discharge? Anything looking like electrodes?'

'No,' Falcon answered, after switching to the highest power of the telescope. 'But here's something odd. Do you see this pattern? Check back on the earlier images. I'm sure it wasn't there before.'

A broad, mottled band had appeared along the side of the medusa. It formed a startlingly regular chequerboard, each square of which was itself speckled in a complex subpattern of short horizontal lines. They were spaced at equal distances in a geometrically perfect array of rows and columns.

'You're right,' said Dr Brenner, with something very much like awe in his voice. 'That's just appeared. And I'm afraid to tell you what I think it is.'

'Well, I have no reputation to lose – at least as a biologist. Shall I give my guess?'

'Go ahead.'

'That's a large meter-band radio array. The sort of thing they used back at the beginning of the twentieth century.'

'I was afraid you'd say that. Now we know why it gave such a massive echo.'

'But why has it just appeared?'

'Probably an after-effect of the discharge.'

'I've just had another thought,' said Falcon, rather slowly. 'Do you suppose it's *listening* to us?'

'On this frequency? I doubt it. Those are meter – no, *decameter* antennas – judging by their size. Hmm . . . that's an idea!'

Dr Brenner fell silent, obviously contemplating some new line of thought. Presently he continued: 'I bet they're tuned to the radio outbursts! That's something nature never got around to doing on Earth . . . We have animals with sonar and even electric senses, but nothing ever developed a radio sense. Why bother where there was so much light?

'But it's different here. Jupiter is *drenched* with radio energy. It's worth while using it – maybe even tapping it. That thing could be a floating power plant!'

A new voice cut into the conversation.

'Mission Commander here. This is all very interesting, but there's a much more important matter to settle. *Is it intelligent?* If so, we've got to consider the First Contact directives.'

'Until I came here,' said Dr Brenner, somewhat ruefully, 'I would have sworn that anything that could make a short-wave antenna system *must* be intelligent. Now, I'm not sure. This could have evolved naturally. I suppose it's no more fantastic than the human eye.'

'Then we have to play safe and assume intelligence. For the present, therefore, this expedition comes under all the clauses of the Prime directive.'

There was a long silence while everyone on the radio circuit absorbed the implications of this. For the first time in the history of space flight, the rules that had been established through more than a century of argument might have to be applied. Man had – it was hoped – profited from his mistakes on Earth. Not only moral considerations, but also his own self-interest demanded that he should not repeat them among the planets. It could be disastrous to treat a superior intelligence as the American settlers had treated the Indians, or as almost everyone had treated the Africans . . .

The first rule was: keep your distance. Make no attempt to

approach, or even to communicate, until 'they' have had plenty of time to study you. Exactly what was meant by 'plenty of time', no one had ever been able to decide. It was left to the discretion of the man on the spot.

A responsibility of which he had never dreamed had descended upon Howard Falcon. In the few hours that remained to him on Jupiter, he might become the first ambassador of the human race.

And *that* was an irony so delicious that he almost wished the surgeons had restored to him the power of laughter.

7. PRIME DIRECTIVE

It was growing darker, but Falcon scarcely noticed as he strained his eyes towards that living cloud in the field of the telescope. The wind that was steadily sweeping *Kon-Tiki* around the funnel of the great whirlpool had now brought him within twelve miles of the creature. If he got much closer than six, he would take evasive action. Though he felt certain that the medusa's electric weapons were short ranged, he did not wish to put the matter to the test. That would be a problem for future explorers, and he wished them luck.

Now it was quite dark in the capsule. That was strange, because sunset was still hours away. Automatically, he glanced at the horizontally scanning radar, as he had done every few minutes. Apart from the medusa he was studying, there was no other object within about sixty miles of him.

Suddenly, with startling power, he heard the sound that had come booming out of the Jovian night – the throbbing beat that grew more and more rapid, then stopped in mid-crescendo. The whole capsule vibrated with it like a pea in a kettledrum.

Falcon realized two things almost simultaneously during the sudden, aching silence. *This* time the sound was not coming from thousands of miles away, over a radio circuit. It was in the very atmosphere around him.

The second thought was even more disturbing. He had quite forgotten – it was inexcusable, but there had been other apparently more important things on his mind – that most of the sky above him was completely blanked out by *Kon-Tiki*'s gasbag. Being lightly silvered to conserve its heat, the great balloon was an effective shield both to radar and to vision.

He had known this, of course; it had been a minor defect of the design, tolerated because it did not appear important. It seemed very important to Howard Falcon now – as he saw that fence of gigantic tentacles, thicker than the trunks of any tree, descending all around the capsule.

He heard Brenner yelling: 'Remember the Prime directive! Don't alarm it!' Before he could make an appropriate answer that overwhelming drumbeat started again and drowned all other sounds.

The sign of a really skilled test pilot is how he reacts not to foreseeable emergencies, but to ones that nobody could have anticipated. Falcon did not hesitate for more than a second to analyse the situation. In a lightning-swift movement, he pulled the rip cord.

That word was an archaic survival from the days of the first hydrogen balloons; on *Kon-Tiki*, the rip cord did not tear open the gasbag, but merely operated a set of louvres around the upper curve of the envelope. At once the hot gas started to rush out; *Kon-Tiki*, deprived of her lift, began to fall swiftly in this gravity field two and a half times as strong as Earth's.

Falcon had a momentary glimpse of great tentacles whipping upward and away. He had just time to note that they were studded with large bladders or sacs, presumably to give them buoyancy, and that they ended in multitudes of thin feelers like the roots of a plant. He half expected a bolt of lightning – but nothing happened.

His precipitous rate of descent was slackening as the atmosphere thickened and the deflated envelope acted as a parachute. When *Kon-Tiki* had dropped about two miles, he felt that it was safe to close the louvres again. By the time he had restored buoyancy and was in equilibrium once more, he had lost another mile of altitude and was getting dangerously near his safety limit.

He peered anxiously through the overhead windows, though he did not expect to see anything except the obscuring bulk of the balloon. But he had sideslipped during his descent, and part of the medusa was just visible a couple of miles above him. It was much closer than he expected – and it was still coming down, faster than he would have believed possible.

Mission Control was calling anxiously. He shouted: 'I'm OK – but it's still coming after me. I can't go any deeper.'

That was not quite true. He could go a lot deeper – about one hundred and eighty miles. But it would be a one-way trip, and most of the journey would be of little interest to him.

Then, to his great relief, he saw that the medusa was levelling off, not quite a mile above him. Perhaps it had decided to approach this strange intruder with caution; or perhaps it, too, found this deeper layer uncomfortably hot. The temperature was over fifty degrees centigrade, and Falcon wondered how much longer his life-support system could handle matters

Dr Brenner was back on the circuit, still worrying about the Prime directive.

'Remember – it may only be inquisitive!' he cried, without much conviction. 'Try not to frighten it!'

Falcon was getting rather tired of this advice and recalled a TV discussion he had once seen between a space lawyer and an astronaut. After the full implications of the Prime directive had been carefully spelled out, the incredulous spacer had exclaimed: 'Then if there was no alternative, I must sit still and let myself be eaten?' The lawyer had not even cracked a smile when he answered: 'That's an *excellent* summing up.'

It had seemed funny at the time; it was not at all amusing now.

And then Falcon saw something that made him even more unhappy. The medusa was still hovering about a mile above him – but one of its tentacles was becoming incredibly elongated, and was stretching down towards *Kon-Tiki*, thinning out at the same time. As a boy he had once seen the funnel of a tornado descending from a storm cloud over the

Kansas plains. The thing coming towards him now evoked vivid memories of that black, twisting snake in the sky.

'I'm rapidly running out of options,' he reported to Mission Control. 'I now have only a choice between frightening it – and giving it a bad stomach-ache. I don't think it will find *Kon-Tiki* very digestible, if that's what it has in mind.'

He waited for comments from Brenner, but the biologist remained silent.

'Very well. It's twenty-seven minutes ahead of time, but I'm starting the ignition sequencer. I hope I'll have enough reserve to correct my orbit later.'

He could no longer see the medusa; once more it was directly overhead. But he knew that the descending tentacle must now be very close to the balloon. It would take almost five minutes to bring the reactor up to full thrust . . .

The fuser was primed. The orbit computer had not rejected the situation as wholly impossible. The air scoops were open, ready to gulp in tons of the surrounding hydrohelium on demand. Even under optimum conditions, this would have been the moment of truth – for there had been no way of testing how a nuclear ramjet would *really* work in the strange atmosphere of Jupiter.

Very gently something rocked *Kon-Tiki*. Falcon tried to ignore it.

Ignition had been planned at six miles higher, in an atmosphere of less than a quarter of the density and thirty degrees cooler. Too bad.

What was the shallowest dive he could get away with, for the air scoops to work? When the ram ignited, he'd be heading towards Jupiter with two and a half g's to help him get there. Could he possibly pull out in time?

A large, heavy hand patted the balloon. The whole vessel bobbed up and down, like one of the Yo-Yo's that had just become the craze on Earth.

Of course, Brenner *might* be perfectly right. Perhaps it was just trying to be friendly. Maybe he should try to talk to it over the radio. Which should it be: 'Pretty pussy'? 'Down,

Fido'? Or 'Take me to your leader'?

The tritium-deuterium ratio was correct. He was ready to light the candle, with a hundred-million-degree match.

The thin tip of the tentacle came slithering around the edge of the balloon some sixty yards away. It was about the size of an elephant's trunk, and by the delicate way it was moving appeared to be almost as sensitive. There were little palps at its end, like questing mouths. He was sure that Dr Brenner would be fascinated.

This seemed about as good a time as any. He gave a swift scan of the entire control board, started the final four-second ignition count, broke the safety seal, and pressed the JETTISON switch.

There was a sharp explosion and an instant loss of weight. *Kon-Tiki* was falling freely, nose down. Overhead, the discarded balloon was racing upward, dragging the inquisitive tentacle with it. Falcon had no time to see if the gasbag actually hit the medusa, because at that moment the ramjet fired and he had other matters to think about.

A roaring column of hot hydrohelium was pouring out of the reactor nozzles, swiftly building up thrust – but *towards* Jupiter, not away from it. He could not pull out yet, for vector control was too sluggish. Unless he could gain complete control and achieve horizontal flight within the next five seconds, the vehicle would dive too deeply into the atmosphere and would be destroyed.

With agonizing slowness – those five seconds seemed like fifty – he managed to flatten out, then pull the nose upward. He glanced back only once and caught a final glimpse of the medusa, many miles away. *Kon-Tiki*'s discarded gasbag had apparently escaped from its grasp, for he could see no sign of it.

Now he was master once more – no longer drifting helplessly on the winds of Jupiter, but riding his own column of atomic fire back to the stars. He was confident that the ramjet would steadily give him velocity and altitude until he had reached near-orbital speed at the fringes of the atmosphere. Then, with a brief burst of pure rocket power, he would regain the freedom of space.

Halfway to orbit, he looked south and saw the tremendous enigma of the Great Red Spot – that floating island twice the size of Earth – coming up over the horizon. He stared into its mysterious beauty until the computer warned him that conversion to rocket thrust was only sixty seconds ahead. He tore his gaze reluctantly away.

'Some other time,' he murmured.

'What's that?' said Mission Control. 'What did you say?'

'It doesn't matter,' he replied.

8. BETWEEN TWO WORLDS

'You're a hero now, Howard,' said Webster, 'not just a celebrity. You've given them something to think about – injected some excitement into their lives. Not one in a million will actually travel to the Outer Giants, but the whole human race will go in imagination. And that's what counts.'

'I'm glad to have made your job a little easier.'

Webster was too old a friend to take offence at the note of irony. Yet it surprised him. And this was not the first change in Howard that he had noticed since the return from Jupiter.

The Administrator pointed to the famous sign on his desk, borrowed from an impressario of an earlier age: ASTONISH ME!

'I'm not ashamed of my job. New knowledge, new resources – they're all very well. But men also need novelty and excitement. Space travel has become routine: you've made it a great adventure once more. It will be a long, long time before we get Jupiter pigeonholed. And maybe longer still before we understand those medusae. I still think that one *knew* where your blind spot was. Anyway, have you decided on your next move? Saturn, Uranus, Neptune – you name it.'

'I don't know. I've thought about Saturn, but I'm not really needed there. It's only one gravity, not two and a half like Jupiter. So men can handle it.'

Men, thought Webster. He said 'men'. He's never done that before. And when did I last hear him use the word 'we'? He's changing, slipping away from us . . .

'Well,' he said aloud, rising from his chair to conceal his slight uneasiness, 'let's get the conference started. The cameras are all set up and everyone's waiting. You'll meet a lot of old friends.'

He stressed the last word, but Howard showed no response. The leather mask of his face was becoming more and more difficult to read. Instead, he rolled back from the Administrator's desk, unlocked his undercarriage so that it no longer formed a chair, and rose on his hydraulics to his full seven feet of height. It had been good psychology on the part of the surgeons to give him that extra twelve inches, to compensate somewhat for all that he had lost when the *Queen* ha crashed.

Falcon waited until Webster had opened the door, then pivoted neatly on his balloon tyres and headed for it at a smooth and silent twenty miles an hour. The display of speed and precision was not flaunted arrogantly; rather, it had become quite unconscious.

Howard Falcon, who had once been a man and could still pass for one over a voice circuit, felt a calm sense of achievement – and, for the first time in years, something like peace of mind. Since his return from Jupiter, the nightmares had ceased. He had found his role at last.

He now knew why he had dreamed about that superchimp aboard the doomed *Queen Elizabeth*. Neither man nor beast, it was between two worlds; and so was he.

He alone could travel unprotected on the lunar surface. The life-support system inside the metal cylinder that had replaced his fragile body functioned equally well in space or under water. Gravity fields ten times that of Earth were an inconvenience, but nothing more. And no gravity was best of all . . .

The human race was becoming more remote, the ties of kinship more tenuous. Perhaps these air-breathing, radiation-sensitive bundles of unstable carbon compounds had no right beyond the atmosphere; they should stick to their natural homes – Earth, Moon, Mars.

Some day the real masters of space would be machines, not men – and he was neither. Already conscious of his destiny, he took a sombre pride in his unique loneliness – the first immortal midway between two orders of creation.

He would, after all, be an ambassador; between the old and the new – between the creatures of carbon and the creatures of metal who must one day supersede them.

Both would have need of him in the troubled centuries that lay ahead.

February 1971